DELERE

This paperback edition first published in 2014 by Delere Press LLP

Text copyright © Jennifer Hope Davy
Unless otherwise noted, all images copyright ©
Jennifer Hope Davy

First published in 2014 by Delere Press LLP

Delere Press LLP
370G Alexandra Road #09-09
Singapore 159960
www.delerepress.com

Delere Press LLP Reg No. T11LL1061K

ISBN 978-981-07-9143-8

# PEDESTRIAN STORIES

By

jennifer hope davy

DELERE PRESS

# Acknowledgements

The artist is most grateful to Jeremy Fernando and his openness to accept the reading of these tales, to be both a blind and seeing reader, and to appreciate the art of storytelling, reading and writing. She also would like to thank him, Yanyun Chen and Delere Press for their enthusiasm and commitment to producing projects they believe in.

Furthermore, she would like to thank all of those who made each tale possible through opportunity, support and inspiration:

A great, great thank you is extended to Jan Kage (Yaneq) for the opportunity to occupy a room for twenty-four hours, which helped to initiate this project. As well, the artist wishes to thank the following people for their background support during this process: Kim Collmer, Ashley Davy Donayre, Julia Hölzl, Anette Schäfer and Miles Chalcraft, and Lisa Wade.

Much love and grateful thanks to directors Claudio Cocuzzo and Giuseppe Lana of BOCS for the wonderful opportunity and support. The artist is also most grateful to the following people for their background support during her residency in Sicily: Johannes Buss, Helena Cantone, Kim Collmer, Giusi Diana, Ashley Davy Donayre, Linda and Ed Fallon, Julia Hölzl, Gianluca Lombardo, Lab. Mammasonica, Martina Marta, Manuela Panebianco, Pepe, Katiuscia Pompili and Lisa Wade. And enormous gratitude to the translation of the text from English to Italian by Marco Tognato, a translation experience that was ever joyful and fulfilling.

Lastly, warm wishes and thanks to director Kyo of the Reading Room for her generosity and enthusiasm. As well, she would like to thank Christian Hänggi for his creativity and humor, Foyfon Chaimongkol for her drawing support, and to all Anon(s) who participated full of surprises and inspiration.

# Introduction

*pedestrian stories* (1-3) began as a singular project consisting of the generation of a short story with images produced in/as a durational performance. The project has now developed into a series come to be called, *pedestrian stories*. Technically, the project involves mostly writing, within constraints. The constraints of which lend itself towards the performative in that a story is to be produced, outside the confines of the artist's domain, within twenty-four hours in which time, the immediate environment and surroundings, the internet, the artist's image archive, and images taken in-situ may become possible players, characters and/or participants in the final production of the piece. Given the twenty-four hour time frame, as a structural apparatus, the series will seek to complete itself in twenty-four stories. For now, there are three and they are here to be read.

Kunstraum Bethanian, 5:30am 5 june 2012

The initial story, *while waiting*, 2012, was produced during a "24hour residency," (which also helped to create the initial constraint) upon the invitation of critic/curator Jan Kage of Berlin for his exhibition at the Kunstraum Kreuzberg/Bethanien. Kage chose to leave one of the exhibition rooms open as a continuous revolving space for a "daily" artist to work or perform each day. Thus for every new twenty-four hours, the space, and its daily artist, negotiated between a public and private environment and utility—part atelier, part exhibition display.

BOCS, 3:30am  20 september 2012

*via grimaldi*, 2012, is the second in the series. This work was generated in conjunction with a larger project and exhibition entitled, *castrato: cuts from a scene*, which was produced during a BOCS artist residency in Sicily. During the residency the artist staged a twenty-four hour performance in which to generate an in-situ story that while standing on its own, also became the residency's co-inspired narrative for the artist's installation. (The artist would like to note that there was some additional, minor, editing performed by the artist after the performance while working with the translator, Marco Tognato, for the purpose of generating a coherent Italian version).

Reading Room, Bangkok  10:08pm  9 March 2013

The third in the series, *in-between places*, was generated in 2013 at the Reading Room in Bangkok. In this particular inception, the project opened itself to voluntary participation from the public, whether in-person during a visit to the Reading Room or online in the open document of the Reading Room website where the writing was taking place. The original version of this open participation piece can be accessed at http://readingroombkk.org/events/in-between-places/. For the story here that concludes this initial collection, *in-between places*, was further edited for the sake of this collective publication. Given that the participatory aspect of the story was a deviation from the original constraints and that much of the noted ideas and trajectory of the piece had yet to evolve within the 24hour collective period, the artist chose to "fill-in" over a 12hour period—alone—for the purposes of this publication (a seemingly acceptable exception). Therefore, the final version to be read in this collection is comprised of a 24hour performance with collective activity and participation, as well as an added 12hours of solitude.

Lastly, on formalities, in this collective gathering of the first three stories additional copy-editing was performed by the keen and sharp hand of Delere Press Editor, Jeremy Fernando, to maintain the quality and standard of their publications. Otherwise, all of the works were originally produced and edited insitu by the artist within their constraints as stipulated above.

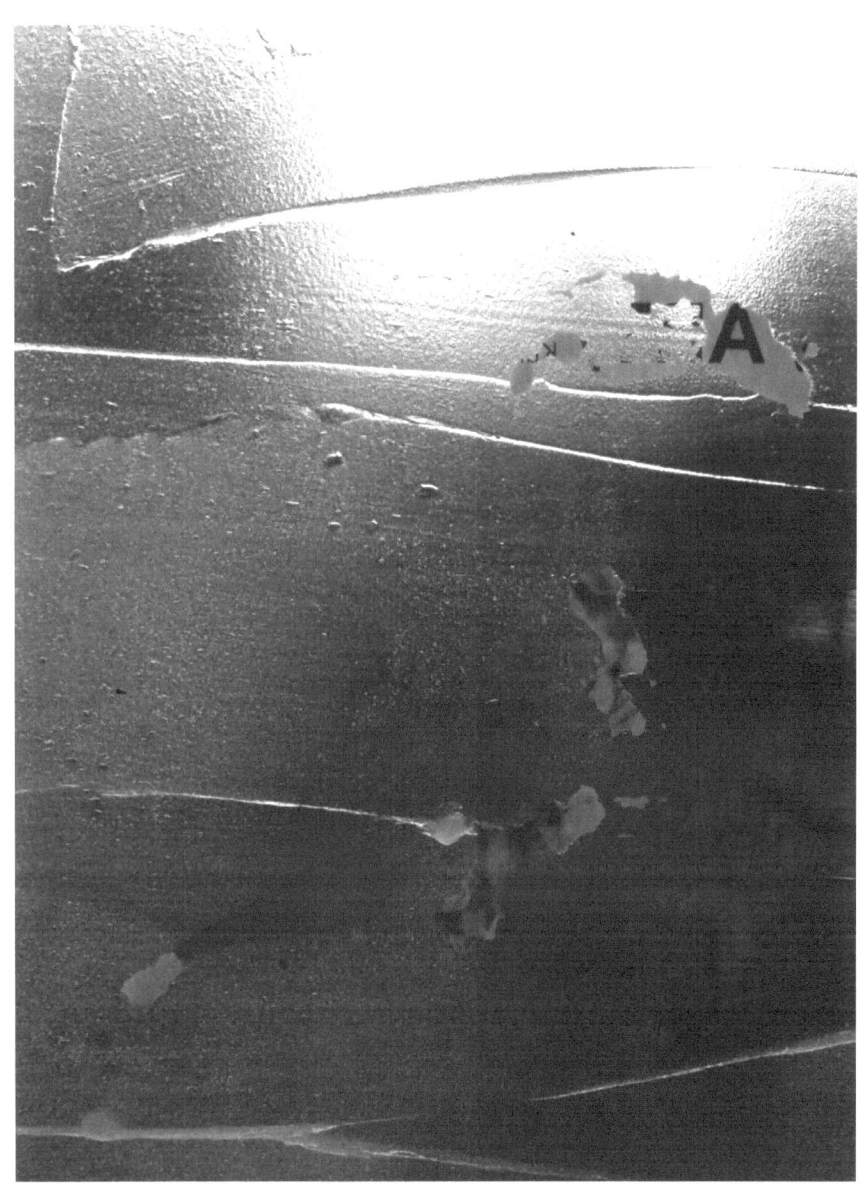

*while waiting*

There was something about the generic brand of "vaseline" that didn't hold up against the real thing—*Vaseline*. Although, admittedly, she couldn't very well answer, in earnest, if she'd remotely even know the difference in a blind test case between the 'real' thing and the close to the real thing; it was really just a hunch. Though presuming her hunch had any weight, the disparity would center on the difference in viscosity—namely that the name brand was more viscous. And as a name it certainly functions better than "petroleum jelly." Regardless of the organic nature of petroleum over that of the less freely occurring jelly, the two aren't necessarily the most harmonic semantic pairing.

Smearing away the rash on a baby's bottom was the utilitarian way that Vivian, among countless others, had first come to know the material, the brand. Aside from this nascence model that Vaseline carries with— its infantile marketing—the contrary comes with, remaining a popular material for the same geographic region of the body. Either way, Vaseline is a product that seeks to relieve pain—before and/or after. Like a slip, which one could think both in terms of casting as well as undergarments, Vaseline provides an extra layer (that extra layer) in between things that both soothes and protects, as well as allows for a certain mobility.

Vivian had gotten in the habit of smearing Vaseline on the front facing windows of the old clap board farm house she and her sister were currently residing in before taking a trip into town. Presumably it was to obscure the view, given the town's propensity for gossip, there were times she felt paranoid about the peculiar conditions of the house. The translucency of the Vaseline was such that it allowed for the ongoing passage of light and color (the latter depending on how thick or thin it was applied), while obscuring visibility in an aesthetically pleasing and subtle way. The whole endeavor was truly a satisfying process for her. Aside from her simply having a viscous fetish, Vivian loved the sound that was created between the metal bladed putty knife, the petroleum jelly and the old window glass—that very tender glass that often seems as though it were made from an antique wine glass rolled out and gingerly fitted into place. There was so much ambient noise in the stillness and quietness of being in the middle of nowhere that the gliding and scraping sounds of her knife was, each time, like an incision, a rhythmically solo incising the din of dry air.[1] She couldn't faithfully recall how it all started, this love affair with Vaseline,[2] except that she had become intimate with it since moving in to care for the Grundsteins, a now elderly couple, and their homestead on the plains of Iowa about a year ago. For sure it was in part simply because it was always there,[3] always on hand or in hand, as the Grundstein's

1 Of course Vivian thought of how this action of hers could be transposed into a performance somewhere in a gallery like setting yet by then, by the end of setting the possibility of that staging, it seemed already over and redundant, losing any sense of the poetic simplicity of the action itself in the moment of its happening.

2 This is probably not entirely true as it wasn't like she didn't recall having done that sound installation in California years prior, the backdrop of which was Vaseline smeared windows. This recollection often failed her though because the idea of 'vaseline on window' she'd in fact stolen and had never really lived it down (for herself).

3 Though it was plentiful, and essentially free, Viv would never use it for herself, not even to assist her dildo's passage—not only were there just too many outside connotations, she firmly believed in drawing certain lines if only for superficial delineation. Viv had come accustomed to K-Y and was brand-loyal. She would in fact go out of her way, literally and financially, to purchase it and only the brand name brand, K-Y. This even after a friend of hers had made the unfortunate remark that it was ironic that Krispin's*, Vivian's x-boyfriend, new girlfriend was called Yeller**. [*Not only were Krispin's parents in love with the actor Crispin Glover, but they had given birth to him prematurely while on a trip to Berlin in which the only undubbed movie available on their hotel room television was "Back to the Future." Given the circumstances, the naming became immanent while the spelling was the result of a Germanic phonetic translation at the hospital and all documents spelled the newborn's name with a K.]; [**Her name was actually Yellena, but Vivian thought is was more appropriate and fun to call her Yeller, as in "Old Yeller" the name of the dog in the book cum film of the same name. Her reasoning behind such uncharacteristic cattiness was her thought that he'd mythologized the new girl as his hero, the savior of his almost middle-aged life, and he did just have a thing for dogs].

in their immobility often seemed plagued with elderly diaper rash. It was probably a good thing the couple was well into dementia. Neither one of them would have tolerated their protracted dissolution. It's not that they'd ever been so overwhelmed with pride that they'd shun assistance or guidance, it was more that they believed in time, or rather timing, and not prolonging it. Every Sunday the two would be the first of the congregation to take their seat, always in the second row leaving prominent space for those to come. They'd also be the first to take their leave as faith was not something to deliberate about—faith was faith, however blind. Such characteristic sensibility was as yet unknown to Vivian and her sister, Portia. For them, the Grundsteins, and their homestead, were merely an escape vehicle paid for by the Grundstein sons whose lives were taking place in the metropolis.[4]

Vivian had also been using Vaseline in between the floorboards to seal over the cracks filled with waste. The project, or rather project materials, the two girls were also being paid to repair the old farmhouse, began, as

---

4 Metropolis here refers to Chicago then Frankfurt. The two boys had gone to Chicago to study, both receiving their degrees in economics from the University of Chicago (economically referred to as the Chicago School). The Elder sought to recover his Germanic heritage and took a job in Frankfurt solely for its proximity. The younger eventually followed in his brother's footsteps, but for entirely different reasons; he'd become obsessed with the idea of a world currency, that would still advocate a price theory-based regulation, and was convinced it should originate in the land of Luther, perhaps for its self-conscious conservatism. How this squared with particular city/states in the list of seven financial governing power areas he'd relegated, which included Beijing, Hong Kong, Tokyo and Dubai, wasn't quite clear to anyone yet, nor it seemed to the Younger himself.

Hans Holbein the Younger, *Lais of Corinth*, 1526 Limewood, 34.6 × 26.8
Kunstmuseum Basel

many things do, by accident. Working together, the sisters were tending to the Grundsteins' diaper change. Portia was holding up Mr. Grundstein while Vivian quickly withdrew his diaper in exchange for a fresh one. In the moment of exchange Vivian lost her balance and the used diaper hit the floor with the contents side facing down. Unfortunately it was a rather large and loose stool that conveniently was now lying over a large crevice in the old wooden floorboards. There was nothing she could do in that moment as Portia's arms were giving way to the durational weight of Mr. Grundstein's gravity bound body. Vivian quickly attended to the new diaper, after cleaning his messy brittle ass though skipping the application of Vaseline to his red, chafed cheeks given the situation. Once he was cleaned up and wrapped up again, the sisters lifted him up together each using a hand to hold him and a hand to pull up his trousers and slip-up the attached suspenders. Seated back down again, Portia wheeled him in the direction of the back door.

Mrs. Grundstein had already been relocated to a rocking chair on the front porch. It was always an awkward moment after changing—it was as if with each changing the Grundsteins lost another morsel of dignity. From the beginning they both would request to be relocated, separately, and it had thus become routine. Mrs. Grundstein preferred the front of the house, to rock in the rocking chair and let humiliation drift off into the wind. Preferring a back door escape, Mr. Grundstein would fight Portia's wheeling guidance to arrive at the barn alone. There he would sit in quiet murmur with his animals, taking stock.

Post-changing hour inevitably offered Portia the surface to wax endlessly about the profound difference between the death years of the animal versus that of the human,[5] the animal being much more capable and efficient, and hence profound, in its death, or dying. "Take cats for instance," she never tired of this example, "they typically sense when they are terminally ill and are going to die therefore they wander off in solitude to pass on."[6] "That is undeniably more sensible and humane then the human animal's relentless attempts at prolonging their mortal existence no matter how pathetic and vegetative a state." It wasn't that Vivian didn't agree with Portia, she just understood the human condition as a more nuanced and complex situation, especially in light of mortality as it is one of the few species whose culture centers around death, their own death(s).

5  Of course to demarcate a particular block of time or phase of life as "the death years" is arguably impossible and this would become a reoccurring argument between the sisters. One could say at a certain "point" one may enter into a phase in which one is 'literally' dying, but otherwise how else is living and dying not essentially the same, biologically or philosophically. Unless we gather round the notion of a period of "ripeness"—that there's a varying peak and consequent decline—surely there is, but not always so in the mind.

6  Portia's account is purportedly true yet the cat's desire for solitude and isolation is considered more an act of survival. Its instincts 'require' it to so in order to protect itself from becoming easy prey. Though, with such clarity now in tact one could continue the argument surely in the human animal and the thought of one's dissolution as becoming "easy prey." Yet humans are primarily a pack animal and care for the other should be implicit, inherent—"should be."

Yes, they both loved animals, though Portia was politically in-love with animals and essentially preferred their company to that of the human variety. This difference in tendency made tending to the homestead much easier for the two sisters with Vivian playing more the role of nursemaid, overseeing the care of the Grundsteins and Portia in the role of the shepherd, tending to the flock of animals still remaining on the farm. When it came to the house repairs both were responsible for working on the house and thus congenially shared the labor.

And so the shitty adult diaper was still lying there, face down on the floor. Neither of them wanted to pry it off to survey the damage. Vivian went into the kitchen and pulled out the Mezcal she'd been savoring since leaving Chicago. "We definitely can't do this without at least one of these Porsch," Vivian exclaimed. Portia knew exactly what she meant and considered the situation a perfect one to don their masks. She ran up stairs to pullout their old Mexican wrestling masks they'd purchased on a trip to Guadalajara. If it didn't shield them from the stench it'd at least make the experience somehow more bearable in its tragic hilarity.

Portia walked into the kitchen, masks in hand. Vivian handed her sister a shot glass of Mezcal and raised hers, "here's to shit!" They both downed their shots in a gulp. Portia handed Vivian her mask, after they'd properly situated and laced up the back of their masks, Portia poured another round and raised her glass, "here's to Grundstein shit!" They downed another and well, a few more, which most likely explains their eventual "genius" idea to take care of the current, and ongoing, situation.

After a deep breath, they walked back into the living room and Vivian, with the stamina of a fighter committed to never give up the ring, picked up the overturned diaper and held it high—"shit don't defeat." Sure enough, the contents of the diaper had fully seeped into the somewhat large crevice in the floorboard.   Shrugging her shoulders, Vivian remarked how bizarre it was that "the colors are almost identical." This sent Portia into a tailspin laughter for a good five minutes during which time she'd knocked one of the jars of Vaseline off the side table that acted as the changing station. Vivian picked it up and went to hand it back to Portia, but held on to it for a second. Portia could see her thinking, she looked at the Vaseline then at the feces filled crevice then back at Vivian and grabbed the Vaseline out of Vivian's hands. Scooping out an enormous sized 'spoonful' with her hands, she plopped it right over the crevice. And with the outside of her sweatshirt sleeve that she had pulled down over her palm with her same fingers, Portia smeared the Vaseline over the crevice until it became level with the floor.

After an undeniably long silence, the two agreed that it "looks fucking gorgeous!" The color was an uncanny match and the Vaseline made it shine in the late afternoon golden light. Portia looked around for the dirty diaper. She picked it up off the side table where Vivian had set it down. Getting down on her knees she angled the diaper in such a way then ran it down the seam of the floorboards from the end point of the crevice down towards her knees. Vivian now seemed in shock, "are you serious?" Portia didn't respond and continued to work: she discarded the diaper (at last) and then grabbed some 'wet-wipes' to pick up the excess fecal matter that hadn't filled the seam, next she took the

Vaseline and with a piece of cardboard from a toilet paper roll ran that over the seam followed by another wet-wipe. She stood up and looked in amazement at how simple and perfect the floor looked, "why bother with all these other fillers we've been using trying to match the floor color, and forget the shellac—its toxic and takes forever to dry."

There seemed to be just the perfect mix of Mezcal that enabled Vivian to see the genius. They'd save an enormous amount of time as well as money. The Grundstein sons would never know the difference and would in fact never even come while they were there as they had yet to ever visit. And, remarkably, somehow, perhaps a combination of the organic food they were eating, the viscosity of the Vaseline and the strength of the wet-wipes, the room didn't seem to carry an odor nor did the crevice or seam appear to attract flies. They agreed to try it out for a while and this seemed to please Portia to no end as she started to digest the countless ways in which this accident proved to be the most cyclical green solution. She had already factored in the functional use of dust and sediment that would accrue and stick to the Vaseline. According to her, this would only add to the concretization of the seams through an organic and sustainable process. Vivian wasn't as convinced, but when she substituted the feces with earth or mud in her mind, everything else seemed plausible. And Portia was right, the amount of waste that accumulated from the diapers was a bit obscene, not to mention the petrol used to dispose of them at the dump in town. Now they could use cloth diapers and when the waste was no longer needed for the flooring they'd switch to fertilizing. Needless to say, Vaseline took on a whole new role in the house and limited by the seams Vivian enjoyed the opportunity to spread out over the windowpanes as well as to temper her mind from the thought of prying eyes.

*   *   *

"Could you grab my purse Portia?" "Let's get going so we're back before sundown."
"No problem love, just help me with the string!"
"Oh, right."
While they rarely left the homestead more than a few times a month, they almost never left it alone. The first time they did they'd realized that Mr. Grundstein was beyond agitated and panicked feeling trapped inside the locked house. The sisters were surprised he'd even noticed, given the couple barely seemed to register much of the minute-by-minute world. Apparently he registered more, especially the sound of the bolt lock which appeared to incite fear causing him to spend countless and fruitless time pawing at the door handle he could barely see or grab hold of, and consequently it probably wasn't all that necessary to lock the door. They had limited mobility in their motorized wheel chairs but mobility none-the-less, so to insure they couldn't get out Portia had come up with the "string theory"[7] to protect Mr. Grundstein, and consequently Mrs. Grundstein. The idea was to make a maze of string in and around the front door in such a way that it would prove impossible,

7  They thought this was quite clever and funny, not least the name.

or fairly impossible, for either Grundstein to get out or get dangerously entangled.[8]

They'd made a "test run" soon after Mr. Grundstein's panic, and apparently the sisters concluded that he actually enjoyed the maze construction or was at least preoccupied by it. While his eyesight was failing, he could touch and sense the varying volumes of space the strings seemed to navigate causing him to renegotiate the space. He'd actually taken to mapping out the mazes on paper.[9] It became a game of sorts and never failed to keep him occupied long after Vivian and Portia got home. Eventually he'd tire, smell dinner and lose interest, all the while Portia would be slowly de-mazing the game.

The Grundstein's could hardly speak anymore. Nor was their sight much in tact. Mrs. Grundstein claimed to still see shapes and colors while her husband could decipher light and dark tones. Without their primary sense in tact they came to rely more on their hearing, though it was diminishing, and the subtleties' of taste, smell and touch. It was one of the most touching encounters the sisters had ever witnessed between the couple, or anyone for that matter, when a few Sundays back Mr. and Mrs. Grundstein had bumped into each other in their motorized wheel chairs. Agitated at first, they tried to get around each other multiple

8  It's not clear the latter was really accounted for in the maze. It seems more to be just luck that neither Grundstein found themselves entangled or strangled by the string theory.
9  Vivian had given them paper and pencils after reading about an art therapy program in nursing homes. Neither of the two had ever taken to the paper and pencils except for when Mr. Grundstein attempted to navigate the maze.

times, but failed. Finally Mrs. Grundstein let out a sigh and started to laugh (however inaudibly, her body visibly laughed). Mr. Grundstein stopped and faced her breath. Then, with part grimace, part grin, he manually worked his chair around hers with his left hand operating clockwise. His right hand at his wife's side was his anchor point tracing her the way as he moved around her. He met her again at the front of her chair. They looked at each other, deeply, for what ever they could see and find in the other. Together they gently began to touch one another and smell the others skin. It was as if meeting for the first time, with only these senses at their disposal. The sincere curiosity and adoration of their attention was becoming epic.

Vivian and Portia stood crippled. They quietly left the house and wandered into the fields. It was still, less for a soft breeze that gently quivered the corn husks and the wind chime hanging from a porch rafter. Between the two a chord progression evolved charting harmonic bars to curry the sister's tears across the plain.

\*   \*   \*

Portia drove this time and dropped Vivian off at the library while she headed over to the feed store to pick up a few specific items for the new calf that arrived a few weeks ago. "I'll see you in about thirty minutes Viv," … "see you when you get here Porsch, say hello to Jimmy and Vic," … "of course!" Vivian walked into the library and greeted Mrs.

Johnson. As always Mrs. Johnson was polite and courteous, but not very friendly. She still wasn't sure what to make of Vivian and her sister or how the Grundsteins could be left by their sons to rot away on a dried out old farm. Vivian often wondered if Mrs. Johnson knew about the floorboard solution, but that would be a stretch given Mrs. Johnson didn't drive and lived only two blocks from the library. She handed Vivian her number for the computer—number two. Number one, Mr. Leaflet, was using the library's sole computer.[10] He turned around and said hello to Vivian promising her he'd be done in about five minutes, "take your time Mr. Leaflet, I'm in no hurry." She knew he'd recently opened up a Facebook account because she'd received a friend request from him the last time she was in the library a few weeks ago. She hadn't yet accepted his friend request because she wasn't sure how much of her Chicago life she wanted her rather anonymous life to share in. Of course now she'd have to accept him right away, as she'd heard that he comes into the library to check his "news feed" daily so as not to miss anything. Of course all that he is not missing now he was missing in spades just a few weeks ago, but its funny how that slight shift changes one's whole sense of perspective. Vivian was no better or worse, her sole reason to check-in at the library was to peruse Facebook—to see if the world out there or in there still has a status.

---

10 It's worth mentioning that Vivian had never received a number higher than two and always wondered if Mrs. Johnson even had any more numbers, if there were ever more than two people in the library at a time, and why there was even a number system to begin with given the tiny population and familiarity among them.

Vivian went over to the 'stacks' and pulled out her favorite book, the one she always pulls out while waiting for the computer. She referred to it as the "voyeur book." It was a small self-published book, somewhat like a comic book authored anonymously. The main character was in fact a voyeur who walked the city streets in search of the ideal, or at least a captivating *mise-en-scene*. And it was structured in such a way that the voyeur was in essence the reader. In one case it was a view into a large family apartment that appeared to be imbibed with idealistic love and joy. Another perspective was that of a beautiful woman and her cat which the author seemed to be more preoccupied with than the other encounters the reader comes across. The pussy section also revealed a slightly more sinister sense at hand in the book; this wasn't simply a journey through the neighborhood. As always, Vivian was struck by the uniqueness of the book and again mystified as to how it ended up (or originated) in this tiny library. And then it triggered her memory—had she in fact donated this book? A friend from Chicago had convinced her to get rid of all her books and get a Kindle instead. She'd resisted for quite a while, she loved her books, but considering she and her sister had decided to 'disappear' it'd seemed like a smart idea to travel with less. That's when she recalls holding on to a few arty or esoteric books, but ended up donating them to the book drive in town soon after arriving—maybe it was hers.[11]

This time though someone had clearly checked it out between her last visit and this one as there was an unknown postcard inside the book,

---

11 Or maybe Vivian was truly getting lost, which is different than disappearing.

perhaps having been used for a bookmark. Vivian slightly gasped when she saw the postcard, "how strange, it's exactly the same image as Mrs. Grundstein's." The old black and white framed picture hung above Mrs. Grundstein's vanity in the upstairs bathroom.[12]

Krankenhaus Bethanien, Postkarte, Rob. Prager, 1912

12 The couple no longer used the upstairs due to their both being in wheel chairs. They did have arthritis, but their wheelchair confinement was due to a car accident in which they'd unwittingly driven through a red light at a busy intersection in Des Moines. They were hit on both sides and due to it being their fault were liable for all damages. It had really been the event that propagated their more rapid decline in body and mind.

She'd wondered about that image, particularly the enormous building that essentially fills the frame. If the image hadn't seemed so fragile she'd have just popped open the back, but never dared to fuss with it given its condition. The one in the book was in better shape and actually had printing on the front which read:

> 884      Berlin SO.
> Mariannenplatz.
> Krankenhaus Bethanien.

She immediately "googled" it[13] and read, via free online translation software, that the 1845/47 building had been a hospital, a Deaconess Hospital, until 1970 in which it was delegated by the Berlin Senat to become an art and cultural center, which it remains as today.[14] Vivian couldn't wait to get back to the homestead and question the Grundsteins, or question them in whatever limited capacity was at hand. "What if Mrs. Grundstein had been born there? Why would anyone keep a picture of a hospital anyhow, and among their toiletries? Maybe she simply found it, here in the middle of nowhere Iowa? They were German though, at least Mr. Grundstein was German, that much we'd gotten out of the Grundstein sons. Oh, right… I was going to look up the etymology of Vaseline."

---

13  Actually she'd used Bing—she was trying to make a conscious effort to share the search engine wealth and since Google had already become a verb it was time to move on.

14  Vivian shuttered at the idea that this could be a "sign" that she in fact should have never dropped that Art Therapy class.

Derived from the German *Wasser* (water) and the Greek *elaion* (oil), it refers to the discoverer's belief that petroleum [cum Vaseline] is produced by the agency of heat and pressure from certain rocks, and the hydrogen of water.

\*   \*   \*

Inevitably, Portia would be late to meet Vivian at the library to head back to the homestead. This would give Vivian an indeterminate amount of time to flip through the old *Vanity Fairs* that populated the magazine corner.[15] More often than not they'd be the same old few, but she rarely got through one cover to cover, so there was always something to keep her interest. It was during her second time at the library that she'd spotted the treasure trove. At first Vivian had been almost scared to pick one up for fear that it would remind her of a metropolitan life she wasn't leading yet there was something about them being out of date, usually at least a few months, that neutralized the anxiety. Reading about life in the metropolis after the fact was just that—it was more like history. It wasn't "happening" because it had already happened and there was

---

15 Another sideline story could develop here—being amazed that the library even carries *Vanity Fair*, as well as that voyeur comic book, Vivian notices one day a torn subscription address label on one of the new/old *Vanity Fair* magazines. She jotted down the bits of information and figured, between the scant town phone book and the post office she could rather easily piece together who was the recipient and consequent donator.

nothing one could do at such point other than to observe, digest, reject and critique. Vivian started to think of them more as *objets d'art*— they were glossy and pretty and even pleasurable. Consequently, they seemed to be a good palette cleanser to the side effects of spending time on Facebook,[16] which she always said "outdates you within the hour, and that's being generous." The whole encounter with these contemporary or present tense archives that represent, or at least symbolize, the 'real world' usually left Vivian a little unsettled, tense and/or conflicted. It was then that she'd get agitated with Portia's tardiness until arriving back at the house, that peculiar zone of freedom.[17]

For the first time, Vivian rushed into the house to see Mrs. Grundstein. She was sitting by one of the windows facing front, one of the windows Vivian had smeared with Vaseline before leaving for town. The pristine gleaming sheen was now speckled with tiny and miniscule morsels of 'air'. Out on the plains of course it was emphatically dusty with varying degrees of particles and debris that fill the air in the slightest breeze. The existence of such is only visible in those shafts of light where air looks like a gravity free dusty snowfall; or made visible as traces of their having been free floating shafts of air as in the windowpanes of jelly—caught like so many prey in a spider's web. Vivian liked to think of the panes

16  Facebook is too easy and obvious a target to cycle through though we make this injunction.

17  No, it wasn't lost on Vivian that in this place that was a peculiar zone of freedom she was ushering death—maybe it was the threshold that offered such freedom.

as constellations of elements in time like various other tiny universes.[18] More often than not this house they'd temporarily tucked into was like another universe, or at the very least a tiny world in progress replete with its own small history that was only just starting to unravel, as any history does, in time. Just the twenty or so minute drive into town often seemed like a world away—a town of 1970 people could just as easily feel like the precipice of the metropolis even though there were miles of empty landscape between it and the next 1970 person inhabited town.

Vivian hurried over to Mrs. Grundstein and after checking if she was ok, asked her if she'd heard of the Bethanien. Again, the women could barely speak anymore, but she murmured something through her pursed lips, which accentuated the strained quality that overcame her face, the backdrop of her sound, as though she were in slow motion trying to decipher a kernel of recollection. "Hey Portia, run upstairs and grab the framed postcard, it's in the bathroom above her vanity," Vivian hollered. Portia pushed Mr. Grundstein in his chair out from the kitchen and positioned him in collection with his wife and Vivian, then ran up the stairs to retrieve the framed photograph or postcard. Vivian seemed a bit dramatic she thought, as though she were living in a story now and they were just on the cusp of finding out a deep secret in the family's history.

---

18  Vivian too acknowledged that it was probably a good thing she didn't get stoned anymore. Portia on the other hand couldn't get stoned enough—to be in-tune and tuned in to the animal world and the land.

Walking down the long narrow hallway upstairs towards the bathroom Portia's eye caught an old family photo—she'd seen it plenty times before of course, but now it occurred like the punctuation at the end of her previous thought. They, she and her sister, didn't in fact know anything about the couple or their family; they simply knew what they needed to know in order to care for them and their homestead. Yet, it was in that moment, just as she turned into the bathroom that she'd realized, as the Grundstein's sons already had, that they really only interacted with them as bodily vessels that simply required maintenance for the interim. Except those few, very few moments, when their humanity was given the stage to be.

Leaning over the vanity she picked up the framed photograph/postcard. Among various no longer used old glass bottles emptied of their contents there were also small figurines made out of corn husks and corn silk that populated the surface of the vanity. Portia had seen them before and thought they were funny little crafty things, something Mrs. Grundstein did probably to pass the time. But why so cynical, they were in fact quite sweet and Mrs. Grundstein surely enjoyed spending her time making such figurines and working with materials at hand. Maybe she'd even started a crafty corn club or had a table at the yearly craft fair in town. Maybe she'd make them as gifts for family and friends. But she didn't make them anymore, she couldn't; she could barely live.

"Portia?" Portia paused and looked out the bathroom window that neatly framed the rows of corn stretching towards the horizon. She recalled one intimate detail the Grundstein sons had shared with she and Vivian.

In their overview of the property they remarked that the lone tree out in the fields marked the end of the property on the southwest side. The tree was kept so Mrs. Grundstein would have a spot to walk out to and watch the sunset. The Elder followed up this detail citing his mother's favorite dream in which she'd "woken up very early one morning and looked out the bathroom window that framed her tree and she saw the sea. She woke up Dad, in the dream, and rushed out to the edge of the fields and sure enough, the sea had come ashore. Dad grabbed her hand and they ran through the gentle waves splashing around before diving in—then waking up." Portia took another look out the window as if she might see the sea, then slowly turned around and walked back into the hallway. She walked very slowly down the hallway, her line of sight more determined at each photograph on the wall. Descending down the staircase, at an even slower pace, Portia looked at the picture of the beautiful old building that was now understood as the Bethanien. It was a hospital, a place that according to the Grundstein's sons Mr. and Mrs. Grundstein never wanted to end up, hence why the sisters were there. Hospitals are essentially over, or under, serviced and over, or under, equipped waiting rooms where miracles happen alongside tragedy.[19]

Mrs. Grundstein didn't seem to have much of a reaction to the photograph—of course she could barely see it if she could see it at all. She felt the frame and attempted to read the framed photograph/postcard with

---

19 Yet why is it that death is considered the tragedy to the miracle of life? Of course loss is the tragedy for the living yet death "itself" is perhaps as miraculous as its birth. Why just live?

her hands. It was clear though that she knew it, knew it as an object, as the frame that housed a particular photograph/postcard she presumably had placed inside the frame at some point and positioned on her vanity in her bathroom.[20] After fondling it for a while, Mrs. Grundstein handed it back to Vivian and motioned, in her very limited physical capacity, upstairs. Vivian sighed.[21] Standing up with the exerted effort of dead weight, Vivian took the frame from Mrs. Grundstein and walked towards the stairs. Following in the footsteps of her sister she found herself in the bathroom replacing the framed photograph/postcard among the old glass bottles and cornhusk and cornsilk figurines.[22]

"Vivian?" Vivian paused—caught in the frame of the fields—every row of corn was perfectly perpendicular to the horizon though they would never meet the sea surely; she too recalled that lovely dream of Mrs.

20  Although, perhaps the photograph/postcard had been given to Mrs. Grundstein already in the frame. Maybe she purchased it that way at a yard sale. It may have been procured in Berlin at the very place it images and transported in a trunk across the Atlantic or it could have been delivered by hand carrier to the remote farm in Iowa. We could take this much further and later it will come up again.

21  This wasn't following her storyline—she so wanted Mrs. Grundstein to sigh, or gasp, then maybe even cry. Then, after a long pause or shed of tears, Mrs. Grundstein would exhale the story (somehow in murmured speech) about spending twenty-four hours in the waiting room in the Bethanien hospital for Mr. Grundstein to recover from his coma or the like.

22  It's also quite possible that those cornhusk and corn silk figurines were not made by Mrs. Grundstein, but rather purchased at the yearly craft fair or made by someone else in town and received as a gift. Yet, it does make the most sense that the objects were made by Mrs. Grundstein.

Grundstein in that very moment, in that very view. Vivian knew it was time, and so did Portia.

"Vivian?"
"I'm coming."
"There's a postcard here from the Elder."
"A postcard?"

Aside from the extremely brief and very business like emails they shared in regards to the business of caring for the sons' dying parents, this was the first rather personal, warm and even friendly communiqué they'd received from one of them. The image on the postcard was of the Euro Bank in Frankfurt. The Elder had lost his job due to the growing Euro crisis, so he stated. In the meantime he'd come up with a "novel idea" and was now selling discounted sausages to, primarily, members of the Occupy Frankfurt movement's tent city headquartered at the EU Bank Plaza. As a result he was becoming a pork enthusiast and had just read about the World Pork Expo to be held in Des Moines, Iowa in the second weekend of June. Sadly he would not be able to make the trip himself as he couldn't afford any major trips as yet, but thought Vivian and Portia might enjoy it and kindly asked "if its possible" that they "take my parents to the Expo or at least bring them back a couple of good Thuringian sausages—their favorite."

It was clear now to both of them, Vivian and Portia, without their really needing to deliberate upon it, that the World Pork Expo in Des Moines would be their last Grundstein task and the Thuringian sausages would be the last Grundstein supper—time *was* becoming waiting.

*   *   *

Indeed, the sausages from the Thuringia dealer were the best the sisters had ever had, although sausage had never been a big part of their diet. Mr. and Mrs. Grundstein ate their pulverized bits of Thuringian sausage although it wasn't clear if they'd noticed the difference. Neither of them remarked when Portia made such fan fare about the special sausages, although Mr. Grundstein did tap his hand on his tray requesting another small portion to be fed to him.

They had timed supper early enough to catch the sunset by Mrs. Grundstein's tree out at the edge of the fields. Portia took Mr. Grundstein and Vivian was behind Mrs. Grundstein. They wheeled the two of them out of the kitchen through the living room where the sun was beaming in deflected blurs on the Vaseline smeared windows. Portia propped open the screen door with her foot and wheeled Mr. Grundstein out backwards then held the door open for Vivian and Mrs. Grundstein. The breeze was just beginning to set in, almost imperceptible without the hint of the wind chimes barely grazing each other in a series of orchestrated false starts. They wheeled over the small grass lawn that foregrounded the classic clapboard farm house and crossed over the narrow dirt and gravel drive. "Tilt back and use only the taller back wheels to cross the ditch," Portia suggested to Vivian. Once in the ditch they both realized they'd have to pivot to pull the wheelchairs up the other side into the start of the cornrows. Though it was only a foot or two below the level ground, there was the slightest shift in temperature, which caused Mrs. Grundstein to shiver a moment. Vivian was nervous, "do you think they'll be warm enough?"

"Of course, I have both of the wool blankets and I thought it would be nice to bring their old bed spread since it has their initials embroidered into it."

"That's perfect. And, well it's supposed to only be getting warmer. It was just a chill."

"And look Vivian, her cardigan is behind her. We can put it on her when we get out there."

"Ok. Help me pull her up first."

It took much longer than they thought it would to travel down the cornrows; the rows are narrow and while the aisles were kept in good shape with hearty solid earth, organic debris would still collect and in certain spots it was difficult to maneuver with the wheelchairs. Still, they made it there before sunset. The sun was just high enough to maintain a glorious white golden light that made it appear as though the land were illuminating itself and emanating such a blinding light that it was in fact the land that caused the sun to glow so strong and bright. It was warm and dry, but mostly warm, not so much as in degrees of temperature as in the atmosphere. It was the warmth of being inside a bubble, literally within the earth's atmosphere, metaphorically as within the warm embrace of one's love.

The sisters maneuvered the couple over the slightly unsettled ground around Mrs. Grundstein's tree and stationed them just in front of the tree, side by side. They'd not said a word, or made a sound, the entire way out there (although that wasn't necessarily all that unordinary). Vivian gingerly put Mrs. Grundstein's cardigan on her and tucked in the blanket around her legs. Just as she stepped out of the sun's way Mrs. Grundstein sighed with content, it appeared. The sun's light had finally made direct contact; she was illuminated and emanating bright. The two were close enough, literally side-by-side, such that Mrs. Grundstein was able to move her weak arm towards her husband's and take his frail hand in hers. He squeezed it tightly and with his other hand tried to shoo Portia, who was adjusting his blanket, away from him. Portia stepped away and looked at the two of them facing the sun—they were bathed in glory. She looked up at Vivian and then at the sun until she started to see those hazy shadowy spots and she turned back to Vivian who gestured for the Grundstein's bedspread. The sisters unfolded it behind the couple and wrapped it around their shoulders tucking it in on each of their outer side. It hung off the back of them rather stately with their embroidered initials centered between them like a family crest.

Looking at the two of them from behind and on towards the setting sun, it was now as though Vivian and Portia had just come upon them—all of a sudden they were intruders. Intruding on a couple, in a time of their own, in a world of their own carved out of the rest and harvested and reaped. Interlocking each other's arms together, Vivian and Portia eased off Mrs. Grundstein's tree smiling with affection towards the figures before them. In their shadow, the sisters bowed slightly forward in a bid of farewell before taking their leave, leaving the couple to wait for the sea.

*Via grimadli*

*male or female?*

*male.*
*but castrated.*

*what?*

*C a s t r a t e d.*
*but, he's unawares*

*. . .*

*oh.*

Maria wanted to castrate herself. She thought. She pleased herself every time she said "castrato". It was one of the few words she'd mastered in Italian, which is saying nothing, and she loved the way it sounded, where and how the emphasis fell, its rhythm—*ka-straa-toe*.[1] For such a debilitating consequence of the word's action, its sound, or sounding, seemed to give much more than it took away. This was the case too, at least for the reception, with the Castrato singers. From what she had read, not only was the Castrato valuable because his singing range remained in tact, but also because physiologically they developed greater lung capacity denying puberty. Castrato is a cutting out, but not

---

1 According to phonetics as suggested by Maria's Italian phrase book. And since we're here, in this note, let it be said that Maria's desire to "castrate herself" has nothing to do with the Freudian protégé, Hélène Deutsch, who believed that the young girl (in her address to Freud's Oedipus complex) developed (passive) masochistic tendencies to achieve her heterosexual role as a women and desires to be castrated by her father. Maria has no idea who Hélène Deutsch is and no she's not just subconsciously blind here either.

a cutting off, before one's time, so-to-speak, in that one never "comes of age" as we say in English. It is an attempt at stilling time, a primary time, just before it begins to ripen and then holding it there—holding that note for as long as one possibly can, like a Castrato.

But yes, *castrato* was the height of Maria's Italian, which is less giving. That the height of her Italian fell on such a word was presumably due to the fact that she was taking care of her friend's dog for a couple months while staying at her place in Catania. And as she was working on an independent project, and essentially knew no one in the crazy yet vibrant city, the majority of her socializing occurred during her daily walks with the dog. The closest 'green' space to her temporary home was the Castello Ursino. It was essentially a straight shot up Via Grimaldi, crossing over Via del Plebiscito and dropping down to Piazza Federico II di Svevia, which is dominated by this great stone medieval castle, turreted on all four corners.

In the otherwise small, unpretentious piazza, the castle appeared somewhat out of place, though upon first meeting one might not question it, especially in a place like Italy, and moreover a place like Sicily. As the layers of time, and conflict, often seem strewn about as though history had been picked up in a tornado, with its remains scattered at whim. In this case, the castle was actually a bit out of place; regardless of metaphor, it wasn't due to a tornado, but rather a volcanic eruption. Mount Etna, that rises, seemingly and unfathomably from the depths of the city that now lie at its base, had its way with Catania in 1669 and what was once a castle above the sea was now a castle relic in a slight depression a few hundred meters from port. Surprisingly, its moat remained mostly intact, which, scholars have observed safe guarded it from ruin.[2]

Via Grimaldi, where Maria had temporarily taken up residence, made the short yet pivotal stretch from the Port area to the castello. It wasn't a main thoroughfare, more a well-worn side street, an effective third class artery that lost its view to the sea due to the economic necessity for grain silos at port.[3] Maria wondered, once, while gazing down Via Grimaldi at the grain silos that stand between she and the sea, where and what exactly would have become of the view from Castello Ursino if it had not been 'naturally' relocated.[4] Now, surrounded by its dry moat and cut off from the sea, Castello Ursino became slightly more of an island than it bargained for.

2 Perhaps it is worth noting that moats date back long before the medieval period, long before Europe, Maria wasn't aware of this at first. Upon first sighting there wasn't even the remotest separation of thought between the moat that surrounded the medieval castle and the medieval castle. It took a happenstance, a guidebook and the internet to coalesce into a distinctive thought of moat—moat—as its own entity. Surely, she's not an idiot and could easily conceptualize and think moat independently, distinct from medieval castle, but for all intents and purposes, for Maria, moat was attached to medieval castle when a conscious division was not taking place.

3 Word on the street, or rather above the street, is that the port of Catania is positioned for a massive renovation in which its industrial complex will be repositioned down the coast freeing the port to cater to an economy of aesthetics.

4 Of course that thought then exceeds the possibility of any real comprehension beyond projected conjecture, as causality or 'recausality' is as nebulous as the lava that erupted one particular day in the 17th century.

Regardless, this island out of place was very much in place, unawares of its own displacement. For Maria, that was comforting as were the friendly meetings among dogs and dog owners—Castello Ursino[5] was a destination. Removed from its source, the castello was an arena where base needs played out—a place to sit, take a time-out, meet a friend or a lover, have a refreshment, walk a dog. Among the dogs, or rather among their owners was always first the establishment of gender— masculine or feminine. The meeting of two females or two males was to be approached with caution or more often than not avoided. It always struck Maria as a strange yet satisfying that it was through the guardianship of an animal that such relationships were formed or not formed; and that through such basic patterns of nature and instincts a set of relationships originate.[6] It was very base and direct, you were

---

5  According to Maria's guidebook, the Castello was built for Frederick II. She also discovered that a Maria had lived in the castle, a Maria that had in fact turned out to be the Queen of Sicily. In large part this was mostly due by proxy, but that was so often the case in such pre and post democratic eras. Maria wasn't as bemused by the 'coincidence' as one might think, but perhaps it was because she'd only discovered it a week before leaving Sicily and thus her reign was almost up. She did ponder, for about a minute or two, while circling the Castello with the dog and her new knowledge at hand, whether or not it would have changed her occasions or her demeanor or her relation, hanging about the piazza. Maybe, but it would have been feigned anyway—a playful projected namesake lineage perhaps only of the spirit. Or would one say "in spirit"? As when one can't not be with you, but says that they are with you "in sprit"… Then, she thought it curious why no one had mentioned her namesake in place. Last, she pondered the awareness, or lack thereof, of the figures of her hometown and that of the island(s) upon which she stood and the thought fast became mute.

6  Sure, one could argue that such is the nature of most all relationships whether it be plant life or intelligent life; Maria did not at all think she was original in her thoughts— she just had them.

either of the right gender or not, and you either had a fair scent or not. It was contingent and fairly simple in that way.

Although Juno, her friend's dog, complicated this simplicity having been castrated. After the now perfunctory period of assessment, there would never cease to be an initial moment of pause and request for clarification. No, it wasn't that she hadn't a clue what *castrato* stood for rather it was more problematic that she did know. "Poor dog" was usually spoken aloud, and concurred. Though, given so, some owners of male dogs would be less cautious and rather than tug their dog away, allow for a trial sniffing out (often coupled with a shrug of the shoulders as though to say, no matter: the dog is neutered, rendered impotent and thus considered mute).[7] Yet Juno's disposition seemed wholly unaffected by the castration, if in fact the castration myth carries any weight, or he was simply doing his best to make-up for his dislocation—so went the story.

The story goes that Persephone found Juno pacing back and forth along the altar at the Temple of Juno in the Valley of the Temples. He had such a domineering presence upon the altar that most tourists shied away from traversing its plinths. Yet his foreboding effect was due mostly in part to his repetitious movement than his actual demeanor.

7  Of course, this dialogue was truly a mute point when it came to female dogs—it wasn't even given a thought. The consensus was that it didn't make a bit of difference for a female dog.

8  Persephone, really? Yes, we know and so does she.

He maintained constant mobility with a rhythmic momentum that made it appear, to Persephone, almost as though it were an orchestrated performance. In reality, the Temple of Juno had essentially just become his domain and pacing the altar was his way of protecting it, otherwise Juno was incredibly lovely at the same time fiercely protective. It must have been Persephone's innate affinity for animals, and perhaps her general sense of love and care, that caused the stray dog to change the course of his momentum towards Persephone, who thus became his new center of gravity. Normally, Persephone wouldn't go anywhere, at least on the island, without Juno, but she didn't want to leave Maria alone in Via Grimaldi, and it was probably just as well given Persephone was spending the summer to help out her mom who'd just taken in a dog and her litter. And well, Juno often got jealous—even in castration.

Ironically[9], it was Persephone's mother, the mother of eight children and really a goddess and mother to all of Agrigento, who'd suggested castration. Demi was considered rather "progressive" by her friends; she didn't believe in myths, mythology or even god (well, maybe a little to avoid being too scandalous). Regardless of her beliefs, or disbeliefs, everyone adored and respected Demi.[10] Alone she'd raised and provided for her children, who all became active members in their communities,

9  Why ironically, because Demeter. (It gets less obvious, hopefully)
10  Maria was in absolute awe of Demi, the degree to which she never shared with Persephone. She wasn't exactly sure why either. Persephone wouldn't mind. Maybe she was embarrassed; on a random list she'd started titled, *other things I'd like to be*, "Demi" ranked high and was in fact the only proper name on her list.

as she had maintained and continued to maintain her community in Agrigento. It goes without saying though that she and Persephone were closest. And between the two, they'd created many a creation myth for Juno, none of which had their roots in a classical canine lineage. In their most recent telling, Juno was a drag queen born of the sea and mistress to Poseidon[11] and ran the hottest summer nightclub in Agrigento—*Poseidon's Wake.*

Both Persephone and Maria had wondered what it would be like to be a drag queen. Persephone often joked about how growing up in a household of mostly boys she often felt like a drag queen.[12] But in reality she was operating more on the level of masquerade—moving through her various incarnations depending on the year or more precisely the day. So too for Maria. Masquerade was fine too, though it seemed to them, only through their dislocated conjecture and fetishizing of drag, that it was a less-embodied act whereas drag occurred to them as something wholly embodied and merely adorned by concomitant masquerade. The "mask" would always be a sterile prosthetic[13] while the "drag" was inherent.

*   *   *

11  The Temple of Juno, Juno's namesake and place of rescue, it was discovered, was actually not dedicated to the God Juno. More recent studies have pointed to Poseidon, but there is as yet not enough evidence to be near definitive. Thus, the Temple remains being called the Temple of Juno, though it's not Juno.

12  If, with any amount of facticity, she could know what that felt like—no, of course not.

13  Ok, here we don't want to get stuck in time on masquerade or prosthetics, but perhaps the in relation to its sterility vis a vis the drag queen, keeping 'castration' in the background, is a fertile provocation, or at the very least, thought.

Of course Maria didn't really want to castrate herself, so much as she wanted to castrate time.[14] "But how would that work? Would it be better to castrate myself from time or time from myself?" She wasn't in search of lost time, or in search of an origin, an originary myth surely, or a new time, also an originary myth, so-to-say. She wasn't searching at all really;[15] if anything she was excavating, experimenting, exploring, but without any specific agenda other than intentionality.[16] Perhaps she just wanted to be, in time.[17] Yet when Maria responded to Persephone's offer to take up in Via Grimaldi while she took a "time-out" with her mom in Agrigento, Maria remarked, "time must be the culprit considering we have to call it a "time-out." For her time seemed like the culprit or to be more precise, mediated time.[18] Regardless, there was some sort of castration taking place.[19] Perhaps it was not so much a cutting off or out,

---

14  And to be honest, she still wasn't really sure what that meant either.

15  Hopefully a relief that it won't be, or will try not to be or become, an interminable lost and found story with a Proustian magic lantern and cookies (to be sure its certainly not a critique against the infamous *In Search of Lost Time*, which is wholly loved by every character here). Yet again, search for 'lost' is not the plan (actually quite the contrary). Though anyone doing anything in this quasi-excavating arena is most likely always staging some sort of search. Maybe art has become that, a search and rescue mission in which of course nothing is really lost except that which is attempting to be rescued or recovered or uncovered (invented) by the artist qua rescuee. For now, it's just a story, always just, and here, it's a pedestrian story.

16  Although, truth be told, that's not what she told people. She made stuff up—to have an agenda. Yet really she was more inline with intentionality as it is "re-curried" in modern philosophy, as far as she comprehended it. It is inclusive of a 'goal' but not necessarily an agenda—they're quite different as she understood it, and wanted to understand it.

17  Though, that doesn't really square with her desire to castrate time does it, or does it?

but rather a cutting forth or a cutting loose, with the genuine hope of an impotent pause.[20]

18  Of course, the next logical question would be, the culprit of what, mediation? Yes, time is mediated and that can be problematic—it causes problems, but its efficient and that solves problems too. She understood this, she'd reasoned with herself.

19  And lets just underscore the obvious here, clearly someone is committed to having castration operate as a metaphor. That's not necessarily a problem, anyone talented enough in rhetoric can turn almost anything into a metaphor. Yet, in Maria's case it does seem sincere, whether or not it remains standing. The word itself, and its meaning, had literally become a part of her everyday lexicon—everyday—and was, again quite literally, her primary word in her Italian lexicon, thus it had been well thought out or at least well thought. So it is not all for naught that she'll weave this play. Furthermore, Maria (and Persephone) believed that metaphor defies the concept—a delimiter—and allows for a poetics to come forth (assuming it's a successful play). Following the space taken out for this note, we might as well address psychoanalysis once more. Clearly Maria's castration metaphor has a relation to a 'general understanding' of castration anxiety in a symbolic sense (but even still, its not really symbolic either). Otherwise it lies in contrast to Freud's notion of castration anxiety, in the literal sense in which he speaks of men's fear of emasculation (and that relates to his notion of penis envy for the girl, both of which are further developed in the Oedipus Complex). In Maria's case, there is a different form of anxiety, if it truly even is "anxiety." Here there is a desire *for* a self-generating castration, metaphorically. In that sense, in relation to psychoanalysis (since that's what is being addressed in this note out of a sense of obligation), the employment of castration is closer to Deleuze and Guattari. Yet "further" still, the metaphor Maria seeks is one of choice: the choice to collectively and consciously make a cut that renders "impotence" agency.

20  As opposed to a pregnant moment, but maybe that's just a vacation, or at least that's how we've come to call it.

Structurally akin to Castello Ursino, Maria was on her own quasi-island at the end of Via Grimaldi. Persephone's house was a large open space tucked away in an inner courtyard in between the blocks of apartment row houses. It had its own small courtyard with high rustic and irregular stonewalls. It also had a small olive tree, which greatly pleased Maria, and due to the setting of surrounding buildings an angular cut-up aperture to the sky. Maria was surprised as to how many stars one could see given she was in the midst of the city, but it was a small city and this upward view was just a few stone throws away from the sea—perhaps that made the visible difference. There was also a long empty garage that connected the small courtyard to the street. It was a nice, clean space, all in light grey concrete. Persephone had re-surfaced it and kept it empty mainly to dance—it had been her first love and she'd always wanted to have a space dedicated to it. Maria would often lie on the cool floor when it got too hot to ponder the empty fullness. The garage door, a rolling door, was typically closed and when kept that way, given the layout of the conjoining spaces, made it feel as though Catania were sealed off from the space. Yet, once the garage door was open, even ever so slightly, the city was just there, and there was contact, and immediate connection. And to be sure, even when the rolling doors were closed the audibility of the city, of the neighborhood, of the neighbors, persisted to permeate—there was really no sure cutting off.

Often Maria wished that Persephone's domain had been situated in the front, located directly on the street with a balcony, like all the inhabitants of the characters she'd come to know lining the street. That way she might feel more a part of the Grimaldi lineage.[21] Yet the configuration was probably better to focus and more emphatically, the distinction between the secluded domicile in the midst of the city and its opposite made the opposite all the more visible, of course. On Via Grimaldi, everyone lived outside, as it was hot, then warm. Whether gathered around the front door in chairs, on a balcony or hanging out a window, there was little desire to remain enclosed.

21  To be sure, she meant of course the lineage in the sense of those that all lined the street and not the Grimaldi lineage of Genoa and Royal Monaco, although that certainly would come in handy. Perhaps the street was named in an homage and hope of the latter.

And stepping out on Via Grimaldi was the animated bridge to and fro for Maria. The road itself often seemed more like a bridge in a passage in time, seemingly out of time yet all the while keeping time. Maybe not as avant-garde as early free jazz, but maybe "more" avant-garde in its being unawares of its own timing. Maria often referred to the experience of walking Via Grimaldi akin to walking the street of a neo-realist film without the still-framed pathos.[22] Yet before being able to punctuate the sentence the reality of its (aesthetic/poetic) forgotten facture spoke out in emphatic exclamation.[23]

*   *   *

22  Seriously, she's not lying. It was the first thing that immediately popped into her head, and of course it was obvious. It is steadfast in the referential lexicon—there's almost no escaping it. What else would come so quickly to mind, in her case, other than what is already contingently there (an index may have a certain absoluteness but it is always contingent, thus this was hers in her case).

23  That the street still holds its own time, in deference to itself or outside itself speaks more to the value of time, or timing and place, or a taking place. Obviously one could not make a neorealist film today, and who would want to? The value of the moment has been produced—obviously, of course—the value is in time; its current value is historic, or 'history'—at auction. Maybe it's the obvious (neo)Marxist thing to say even when Marxist, as a descriptor, was part of its value, then. Keeping in time, again, how does one address such concerns today, aesthetically? Bake bread? Maria had already thought of organizing a film screening by consensus (of course), after a neighborhood clean-up party in the utterly trashed piazza a block away from Via Grimaldi. Maybe she could pass out homemade bread and begin with a lecture series with rereadings of Marx alongside Zizek and Bifo? (PS. This should not be taken as cynically as it may yield).

Agatha, a friend of Persephone's, called to invite Maria to go to Modica, a small Baroque hill town in the Southeast of Sicily. There was a series of cultural events taking place over a twenty-four hour period in various venues of the city. Maria had already known about it from Persephone and though she was feeling a bit tired of organized culture was committed to going.[24] She did want to meet Agatha and surely she would meet some interesting people at the event. They were calling it Vespri[25], or the Vespers, referring to the Catholic, as well as Lutheran and Anglican, prayer services that take place in the evening, named after the Latin word for evening—*vesper*. As well, the occasion referenced the historical, and very significant event of the Sicilian Vespers. It was a very nice use of the word, or term, formally and conceptually as a thematic platform from which to address and present various projects dealing with socio-economic political and cultural issues. The event also employed the structure of theatre for its program; Agatha and Maria had gotten a late start and arrived mid-way through "Act I," a puppet theatre on the steps leading up to the San Giorgio Cathedral. They both loved the piece, even though Maria could barely understand a word[26]—

24 Actually, what she really wanted to do was hop on a boat to the Aeolian Islands and fain glitterati as her guide book had so desirably descried.

25 *Vespri* was an actual event that took place in Modica from the 24th to the 25th of August. For more information: http://www.gallerialaveronica.it/mostre_dett.php?id_m=MTM=

26 Though she'd done her homework; the contemporary piece took the seminal novel by Elio Vittorini, *Conversations in Sicily* as its inspiration (written in 1938, it was a stand against fascist thought delivered through poetic allegory to withstand the censorship), while it met with another dueling narrative that acted as conjecture.

what seemed most poetic, though slightly lacking in enthusiasm, were the puppets staged in the audience who were given voice, through the prosthetic device, to refute, reject, protest the goings on, on stage. The setting surely could not have been more poetic; with the cathedral at their backs they took their seats on the steps facing down upon the stage as in a Greek theatre.

At first she thought it was part of a dream, perhaps induced by all the chocolate the two of them had eaten last night,[27] and she was off in a distant land, but she awoke and recognized the very traditional Sicilian styled tiles that covered the floor of their Modican bed and breakfast, and the bag, now only partially full, of chocolate. She heard the sound once more, and yes that definitely sounded like the Islamic call to prayer.[28] And in fact it was, they found out later, part of an artist's project to recover a space that had actually never been allocated regardless of the history of the population in the region (and in Sicily).[29] Maria woke up about twenty minutes later as Agatha couldn't fall back to sleep and had knocked over her toiletry kit en route to the bathroom. It was just as well they were up early as they decided to spend the day in Siracusa

27  If there were more time there'd be a nice reference here about chocolate, geography, transportation and desire.
28  She did have to admit that she personally had never heard the Islamic call to prayer "live", but from what she'd heard a few times on television, she could decipher a case.
29  The project was produced by Igor Grubic titled *Missing Architecture* in which the call to prayer was recited by a muezzin from Modica five times throughout the day beginning at 5am.

before heading back to Catania. Agatha needed to pick up a text; she was helping a friend work on a new translation of Sappho's poetry, or the fragments thereof, in the Sicilian dialect. This worked out well as Maria had really wanted to see the remnants of the ancient Greek theatre in Siracusa.

They made a small stop in Noto for a granita and a quick walk down the boulevard of Baroque, a rather impressive display of high to late Sicilian Baroque.[30] Both Agatha and Maria felt especially cared for being bathed in the warmth of the sun; and that particular morning sun gave an angelic white light sheen to the glorified buildings, their decorum casting shadows in excessive arrays of exaggerated convex, concave and swirling curves and arabesques like a repetitious and animated mosaic of shadowed forms.

While strolling down the main thoroughfare, the church bells marked ten o'clock and the resounding sound that briefly hung in the air reminded Agatha of the call to prayer she'd heard early that morning. "I didn't tell you about my dream, or what I thought was a dream, then it was like a 'vision,' but of one produced by emanating sound. But then I fully awoke and realized that I was in Modica and that the sound was 'live' and it was someone voicing the Islamic call to prayer!" "Really?" "Yes,

30  The excessive building in the Baroque style on the island is primarily a result of a devastating volcanic eruption followed by a devastating earthquake coincident with the birth of the baroque. The devastation resulted in many areas having to rebuild almost entirely.

isn't that bizarre?" "Yeah, I guess, but isn't there a fairly well populated Muslim community in Sicily?" "Of, course—we're the fertile island in the Mediterranean, everyone has had at least a lay-over here, but still, this country is Catholic with a long shadow, so it was just so out of place to hear it." "Yeah, the call has an incredible ability to transport. The first time I heard it in Istanbul it paralysed me out of place, but at the same time completely present in it. I looked forward to hearing it through out the day not simply because I loved the sound but as much because, even in my ignorance of the Muslim prayer, it 'called' me to pause. Oh, I wish I'd heard it."

Just then there was another interruptive sound, though much more of a gravity call—reminding one of their place on the ground although cellularly connected. It was a text message from Persephone, quoting a young girl she'd just overheard at the archeological museum in the Valley of the Temples:

> There sure are a lot
> of ladies being chased
> around the pots!

\*   \*   \*

Agatha dropped Maria off at the Archeological site and drove into Ortygia to pick up the text. It turned out that her friend had a last minute meeting so had left the text with the guy who runs the café bar below her flat. Rather than join Maria at the archeological park she'd been to a dozen times, after retrieving it she thought she'd take a swim, it was getting hot, and read. Mario, the man behind Mario's Cafe had a thing for blondes, Agatha's friend had forewarned her. Agatha had long blonde hair and the family joked how she wasn't really a member of the family. Her dad would chide her, telling her she'd been left behind by the Normans. This always caused her grandmother to smack him as her story delivered Agatha from 'on-high', a gift from God. She did have an angelic quality with her clear fair skin that moreover was underscored by her demeanor—ever loving, kind, giving and inherently wise. Her father may have teased her incessantly, but she was clearly his favorite.

Mario handed over a large envelope that enclosed the text and offered her a coffee. They chatted for a while about her friend, the busy summer the café was having, which had provided much better business than last year, and whether or not Agatha had a boyfriend, or was she not interested in men… Clearly, it occurred to Agatha, Mario had taken a peak at the documents inside the envelope. Agatha paused and smiled, "I like Sappho." Mario held his breath a second or two longer than usual… then appeared slightly confused, and just before he could suggest their going out later that evening Agatha asked for a bottle of water and the bill. She thanked him for the envelope, and his company, "maybe next time I'm in town we can all go out for dinner."

She slipped into the bathroom to put her bathing suit on, there was a great little swimming spot just a couple blocks away. The sun was at high noon setting the scene ablaze allowing the sea to reflect its deep, deep Ionian blue. Just ahead of the waterfront set among the rocks, there were wooden platforms erected to sun bathe and steps down into the sea. After an immediate drop into the sea, Agatha got contently situated and embraced this small "time-out." She loved this spot because she could either look out to the sea, the endless horizon, or turn and watch the quiet, modest baroque waterfront street and its passersby, all the while being just barely out to sea. Her eye carried from one end, the end of her telescopic ability, to a point where the road turned and disappeared out of sight. All along that path she watched, what she'd always seen before, the repetitious rhythmic patterns of the balustrades and the curvature of the decorative moldings adorning the doors and windows of their houses. In this particular row of buildings there was an economy of details, but enough to accentuate and soften an edge, to elevate or compensate an economy of means. What was it in these particular, soft and sinuous curves that became so omnipresent? What is in a form that makes it bend just so, always at a particular arch? The omnipotence of the arabesque—what is in that trajectory?

Such thought also reminded her of talks she had with Persephone, who'd always wanted to be a dancer, on gesture and movement, and believed that much could be given in the smallest of gestures. And so much has been attributed to the smallest of gestures, like gender. And is that trajectory gendered? Could there be so much in a gesture and how do we come to know such gestures, their form, their repetition? And should it not be taken for granted that in every laid stone or bent iron is a hand. And isn't how these gestures, forms and movements come together a movement of authority as well as contingency?[31] And is it simply an act or a result of contingency that patriarchy is authority? Perhaps "patriarchy" must be cut from its gender and read as a proper name as much as "Sicilian" is understood as a proper name, though not necessarily specific.[32]

31 One could always rely on Agatha to question, question almost anything from the smallest of details. Of course now, in her own head she was questioning herself and wondering if these were all just naïve lines of thought. Really, how would one claim that a balustrade be feminine or masculine outside of language? But of course, language is culture. And, at the same time, how to know difference, patriarchy is imbedded; it is an imbedded culture of patriarchy that we know no other. Even in the realm of the "progressive" class that one assumes is "beyond" (of course there's no beyond anything) Agatha expected more. She was curiously critical of an arts project friends of hers had produced for their artist-run space in Catania. It is titled *Origini* and the aim is to focus on the exchange between center and periphery; inviting artists from afar to live and work in a more rural region of Sicily with the hopes of fostering exchange and discovery. The project has been produced twice; each director, there are two male directors, invited an artist to the village or town where their father's had grown up. Agatha had asked why not the mother's village (because the home in Sicily is with the father) or is the mother's home to be used in the second round (there are no plans for it). Agatha loved both of the male directors and highly respected them and their commitment to art and artists, though the project's assumptions were curious, and again, not even thought—*otherwise*.
32 She'd seen a recent post on Facebook that was validating:
 "The thing is, it's patriarchy that says men are stupid and monolithic and unchanging and incapable. It's patriarchy that says men have animalistic instincts and just can't stop themselves from harassing and assaulting. It's patriarchy that says men can only be attracted by certain qualities, can only have particular kinds of responses, can only experience the world in narrow ways."

She'd been watching an older couple assemble their self-made front terrace—essentially a pole horizontally resting on two metal stands extended out into the street roughly a meter from the façade of their home. It was a beautiful economy of means as were the gestures the two were sharing between each other; she could see even from so many meters away the care of her touch for him. Agatha had lost all track of time, realizing the couple was nestling into their cocktail hour on their terrace, she was sure time must be getting on. She reached into her bag to grab her phone to see if Maria had messaged, instead she'd grabbed the remnants of what had been a perfectly ripe fig she had planned to eat after her swim. She'd forgotten all about it, lost in her thoughts and observations, and had been using her bag as a pillow. Now the fig was 'feeding' everything inside the bag. She was actually really hungry and just started to clean the fig off her phone like a cat, and of course there was a message soon uncovered from Maria sent about 20 minutes earlier—oh Agatha!

Maria was exhausted, mostly from the intensity of the sun.[33] "Sorry just seen your message—on my way!" It was from Agatha. She sat down

---

And that's the thing, it's not necessarily a gender issue anymore as much as it is a cultural issue—a patriarchal cultural issue—in which there is no, as yet, cutting off. Within the same few days she also saw a news photo (from a femme oriented news source) of a woman protesting in Bangalore. She was holding a hand written sign that took the American folk song as a platform: "If I had a hammer I'd hammer out patriarchy."

33  And for some terrible reason, perhaps from walking in the footsteps of the ancient Greek theatre all afternoon, she could not get the climatic theme song of the 80s film *Footloose* out of her head; it makes its debut just after Kevin Bacon's character, Ren, offers his defense for the right to dance to the town council quoting from the bible:

at the little tourist set-up comprised of random bits "Sicilian" and went to purchase a bottle of water from one of the kiosks. The kiosk attendant gave her the water and a receipt for 80 cents, which Maria tried to refuse, there was no need for her to have the 80 cent receipt, yet she recalled this pattern and the seeming necessity that each and every receipt be delivered regardless of its seeming insignificance.[34] But who is to say that that 80 cents is not significant, once each and every 80 cents

"'From the oldest of times, people danced for a number of reasons. They danced in prayer... or so that their crops would be plentiful... or so their hunt would be good. And they danced to stay physically fit... and show their community spirit. And they danced to celebrate.' And that is the dancing we're talking about. Aren't we told in Psalm 149 'Praise ye the Lord. Sing unto the Lord a new song. Let them praise His name in the dance'? And it was King David – King David, who we read about in Samuel – and what did David do? What did David do? What did David do? 'David danced before the Lord with all his might... leaping and dancing before the Lord.' Leaping and dancing. Ecclesiastes assures us... that there is a time for every purpose under heaven. A time to laugh... and a time to weep. A time to mourn... and there is a time to dance. And there was a time for this law, but not anymore. See, this is our time to dance. It is our way of celebrating life. Its the way it was in the beginning. Its the way its always been. Its the way it should be now."

34 It always amazed her the proliferation of receipts, it was a nice touch on the one hand but as well it seemed so excessive at times and she could never get anyone to just not issue her one and if she didn't want one, like at the granita stand last week the person wouldn't take it, wouldn't trash it, would just let it sit there until the wind carried it away. Still, she ended up keeping every single receipt—looked forward to filing taxes with hundreds of 80cent receipts or make a flip book out of them, the flip side (blank side) the drawings to animate the purchase of a small bottle of water (although she'd probably not be filing taxes again that year as she continuously failed to earn enough to warrant the tax form).

is added up it surely could become quite significant. As well, in terms of the interaction between she and the attendant, the majority of it would be taken up with the receipt. It was an integral part of the action, to be typed in, computed, outputted and delivered. There was more action involved in the receipt that it actually made the water, the purchase, subordinate to the generation and exchange of receipt of transaction. It made her think about the interplay between the actor and the chorus in the Greek theatre. On center stage would be the very few actors enacting a rather economical means of the narrative; the details, particularities, and driving forces of the narrative were delivered by a chorus. What would it be like to travel with a chorus, she wondered. To remain slightly removed from yourself, to never have to explain yourself, gesturing here and there, yet just to the side of you was your chorus, with your stats, detailed information, answers to presumed questions—your receipt.

*   *   *

Perhaps it seemed odd, but Maria was happy to be back on Via Grimaldi and with Juno. She'd only be gone a couple days yet the sanctity of what was becoming her island that seemed to be out of time and place provided her with a certain comfort. That first evening back she'd discovered another "island" at Via Grimaldi 41. On her walk with Juno she'd forgotten to pick up capers, she was going to have a try at making Caponata from scratch, so dashed out again without Juno in tow before the shop closed. On the way back, a young boy was hurriedly picking up small objects that had fallen out of a box that he'd precariously wedged into a child's stroller. She crouched down and gestured to help him pick things up, and though he seemed anxious he accepted her assistance.

The items were quite random and clearly used: a car seat belt, a rose colored porcelain brushed vase with a floral relief with interior stains from having carried flowers for a time, a small worn out teddy bear with a USB cable tied around its wrist, a blue and red striped umbrella, a naked plastic doll with slightly tarnished blonde hair, a leather calendar planner (from 2010), an electrical extension cord, an Italian copy of *The Lion, the Witch and the Wardrobe* by CS Lewis, a pair of men's jeans and a pair of kids jeans, a flashlight, a miniature fake plastic olive tree, and well, a few other things including some dishware and silverware, and a picture book about Mars. The latter was quite coincidentally humorous given Maria had earlier just seen that she was 'tagged' on Facebook in a photo by friends of hers "who'd just been to Mars." Obviously they hadn't and nor had she; they were in Los Angeles for the first time and had a day trip to NASA in Pasadena. Maria's cousin worked on the Mars project at NASA and gave them a private tour that apparently left them feeling as though they got as close to driving on Mars as anyone ever would.[35]

35  Incidentally, this experience only had the slight fault of diminishing what could otherwise be a slightly other worldly experience to drive Sunset Boulevard from end to end for the first time.

Twin Peaks, Mars, Photo Credit: Dr. Timothy Parker, JPL NASA

The boy's collection of items was an odd assortment and certainly it seemed as though he'd found such a medley combing the streets and sifting garbage piles. He was happy to have it all back in the box and Maria helped him to better secure the box within the stroller. She thought he couldn't have been more than ten years of age, at the most. His eyes were full of innocence yet not sheltered by it; she had an intense desire to embrace him, but that was probably more a drive that would serve her more than he. Heading in the same direction they continued together down Via Grimaldi until the growing sense that the boy's anxiety wanted to be rid of her caused Maria to slow down a bit and linger, letting him move ahead. She slowly gained on him at Via Grimaldi 41 where he was feverishly knocking at the door. It was a building Maria had thought was abandoned—by all looks of it surely it did not seem all that inhabitable. He looked back at Maria who looked to the sky, to ease his concern, though as soon as the door opened she took in as much as she could.[36]

It was quite incredible, there appeared to be a small village behind those old wooden doors. She caught a glimpse of a small alley, what may have once been a hallway, with small stall-like constructions (with slanted roofs) on either side of it. Those that she could make out had lanterns strung up shedding a bit of light. And she was surprised to see so many people bustling around—it literally was like another village in there. Just before the door slammed shut she noticed inside the night sky above. In this case, the street façade seemed merely just that, seamlessly keeping in line with all the other buildings, yet merely a façade, a shell containing another world inside.[37] In this way, she found it rather

36 She'd then scold herself for this later—for why not let it be? Clearly he had something to hide or something he did not want to share and she should let him have that space, that (attempt at a) zone of freedom. Yet, as well, for the sake of a story, for the sake of revealing another zone, perhaps not necessarily free, but outside, Maria must look inside to see and tell of something else.

37 Here one might suspect a grand thematic interlude, which is certainly warranted and doesn't really need to be spelled out, as the set-up is already there. An analogy and metaphor should be made, whether through a thought had by Maria or perhaps it could occur through a conversation that Maria has on the phone with Persephone or maybe they just send each other a series of text messages. Or Agatha could stop by and she and Maria take a walk down to via Grimaldi 41 to linger about, in waiting, in which while waiting they enter into a dialogue about this other world, this island within an island, all geographically situated on an island whose history sheds light and casts a shadow conceptually and formally upon this other zone of economy and culture. An economy and culture within an overarching economy and culture; the zone that encompasses the call to prayer, the Vespers, that you don't hear, or see. So, this note also becomes an-other space of the "story" (that is not exactly a story) as a device among devices—in brief it is efficient, as this writing is constrained by time, and it is also a chorus, or a silent chorus if one so chooses to overlook.

similar to the convent located a few addresses down the street that she also had trouble accessing.[38] Of course the convent clearly had greater resources—it occupied a large lot that bordered Via Grimaldi and extended down another few blocks towards the Port, though she'd found it difficult actually to determine the exact occupation of the convent given the way the streets were divided and occupied around it. What was most peculiar about the situation for her was that one community island was in the service of serving god and his inhabitants while the other community island appeared to be in need of those services yet somehow the two were cut off from each other though they shared the same city block.[39]

She brought it up with Persephone, who immediately combated her theoretical analogy with what she deemed an "obvious argument": "yes, yes, sure, but you could say that every dwelling is an island off the shores of the streets." Maria agreed of course, and complimented Persephone on her use of language, "yet in these particular cases, which do seem

38  Although this was more due to the fact that the entrance to the convent was located on a smaller side street that was difficult to access, and well, Maria's hours were probably more inline with the gypsy village than that of the convent (though keeping in mind that such a statement is based on ignorant and presumptuous conjecture).

39  And yes this is phrased somewhat naively, perhaps on purpose, or perhaps Maria just wanted to fain naïveté in order to scratch gingerly at a surface as though for the first time.

quite particular and given their proximity… and fine maybe it seems redundant to emphasize, but there does appear a difference in the sense that there is a concerted effort in both cases of a cutting off." "And… I'm still not sure its worthy of emphasis and if it is, what for?"[40] Persephone didn't have much patience for Maria's floating theories or thoughts, which she always felt were tinged with pathos and she had no tolerance for that. She also thought Maria was suffering from, what she liked to call, the "oh, you just got here" syndrome. Conversely, Persephone's intolerance annoyed Maria who thought Persephone overlooked the obvious even when she was pointing it out.

"So did you read my latest tweet?" Persephone had already sent Maria a text message and a link on Facebook all within the last twelve hours, which seemed to defeat the purpose of having a twitter feed especially as Maria was already a subscriber to "Persephoneposts."

> bearded man in 3/4, naked, mantle on shoulders, advances in menacing manner sword in right hand, left hand grabs at a young woman in flight

40  Maria wanted to answer, because she felt it was worthy of emphasis, the fragility (and possible sterility) and the proximity of these divisible lines between two particular zones of culture and economy within a larger over-arching zone that those cultures and economies surreptitiously feed from and/or feed into… but Maria chose not to answer, she could tell Persephone was not interested and/or didn't have the patience for her meanderings. Maybe she was right, and… so… what?

"It's taken from one of the didactic texts for the craters I was looking at in the archeological museum the other day. I think I'm going to continue posting these as a series, what do you think?" Of course Maria had the antagonistic urge to come back at her with, "what for?" but she refrained. "Sure, why not?" Maria was actually more impressed with the content's form of delivery and pondered the future of history in 140 character bite-sized chunks.[41] But it was funny, as was the young girl who immediately realized in the craters the pattern of women being chased 'around pots.' "I actually think it could be a fun project, why not try it out and see what kind of response you get?" Persephone agreed, "maybe restaging history in didactic bytes does something?" "And according to Agatha," Maria added, "we have yet to truly think what a patriarchy is or think outside of it, but I'm guessing that's probably because it's woven into the very fabric of what we wear." "Precisely, and we're already wearing it! I love Agatha, she's the most naïve person I know who's simultaneously wise. Ok, I have to attend to Demi! And she wants to know if you and Juno are coming to Agrigento next weekend, so let us know."

Persephone was not only helping out her mom for the summer, but taking a "time-out" to pursue writing.[42] While she'd always wanted to be

41 Yes of course, this is probably the obvious post historical or pre-post-after-history in the midst of digital-communication-information-immersion thing to say, but really, how could one just leave that little nugget untouched.
42 Actually, she'd been laid off, but didn't tell anybody. Even though her being let-go was purely a result of the company's down-sizing and not her ability, her pride inhibited her from admitting so and she'd go to great lengths to dispel anyone from thinking as such.

a dancer, and loved sharing that fact for some reason, dancing remained her passion, but did not become her profession. In part by accident she ended up doing a lot of writing and editing first in her studies of course, but then began getting good paying work doing it and somehow ended up in advertising. During slow times she started writing for herself, little bits here and there; she started to write a few articles for the local paper and a few essays for a national magazine, and most recently had started to play with Twitter as a platform. Now, that she had this "time-out" she was committed to really trying her hand at writing; she wasn't clear how it would come together yet, whether in essay format or a novel, but she was interested in experimenting with it far, far away from the commercial zone. She was interested in writing as gesture, as in her relation to dance, and as opposed, but not in deference, to narrative. She thought that if she could write like she wanted to dance she might find a place there, in there.

*   *   *

As far as Persephone was concerned, she left the agency to pursue her desire to write and that was the end of the story. If anyone inquired about her financial stability she would state that she'd been saving up for this opportunity (i.e. her severance package) and that if and when the time deemed it necessary she would look into freelance possibilities, to maintain her independence. All in all, it wasn't really that far from the truth.

"Hi P, just wanted to let you and Demi know that Juno and I are coming out for the weekend! We can't wait. And by the way I asked if Agatha wanted to join, but get this, she met some guy who does firework choreography, displays, whatever. Yeah, so much for her hating Sicily's incessant fireworks, she's going to a show he's doing in Palermo next weekend—hilarious! Ok, ciao ciao."

God it was hot, Maria filled another glass of water and went into the empty garage space; she was going to 'channel' Persephone and either dance or write for a while. Sometimes she'd just go in there and open up the garage door halfway, cutting everything off, in anthropomorphic dimensions, somewhere along the torso, and just lie down on the cool floor. It seemed like a productive way of carving out a space of time.

The boys were just in front of the garage door again, which she'd left slightly ajar and it was cutting them off at the shoulders. The opening also helped to keep the breeze moving through the space, in and out through the small courtyard. It was also the best and only way to be directly connected to the outside world yet not be too overly distracted by it. The boys were trading cards, sometime amicably, sometimes not. They were probably about eleven or twelve years old, at the most. Maria enjoyed listening to their banter and barter, and watching them shuffle through their collections to show their most treasured acquisition or trading option.

Most especially Maria liked how they would move to and fro just in front of her as though she didn't exist, and how they could move so motionlessly, and effortlessly, continuously over time. They'd typically position themselves just in front of the garage door—centered, full-stop, as though that had been the destination. This was simply about three meters from their front door, yet here, three meters away, in front of someone else's door they seemed to achieve a greater space of privacy—in that smallest expanse of separation was a cut away from home. They would also begin in whisper—their cards were valuable, all three of them knew it, but eventually the discussions would escalate, presumably over a highly sought after card. Somehow though, seemingly unawares to themselves, they would move back and forth in front of the garage. Sometimes out of view completely, and Maria would wonder if they were just heading up Via Grimaldi, but then she could still here them continuing making their deals just out of sight. It was as if (or, like) they were floating in the water, allowing the current of the waves to move them to and fro with little to no effort or control.

Scala dei Turchi was one of Persephone's favorite places to swim on the island of Sicily. Not only because Demi had taken her there since she was a little girl, but also because the place was so transporting a site. She immediately went for a swim. The Mediterranean was particularly strong that day and Persephone could feel the current pull at her. She knew that if she didn't keep time, keep up a certain rhythm, she'd easily get pulled out to sea without knowing. And precisely because of that realization she cut her swim a little short as she was getting quite tired keeping extra pace. But first, after swimming close to the shore, she lied on her back and allowed the buoyancy of the water to hold her while she took a time-out, letting the sky pass over like out-takes with the sound cut off. Wresting from the waves, Persephone came ashore rummaging around a bit with her hands in the sand to uncover a few good 'rocks' of the infamous mud that amasses in this cove.[43] She found two good chunks and sauntered over to her towel and laid down—she was utterly content she thought, utterly content. Staring at the sun with her eyes closed she reached over to grab her book, finally, she started to wonder how long she'd carry it around with her before getting past the first chapter. A shadow just then intercepted her sun, and it was slightly larger than the book's ability to cast shadow. Leaning up from just the middle of her back, Persephone pulled the book away from its position over her face and looked—it was that guy in the little red bathing trunks. She'd noticed him earlier—he was working on being noticed—on her way to the other end of the beach.[44]

"So, what are you reading?"[45] Persephone exhaled the slightest sigh and

43  Thousands of years of accumulation created the Scala dei Turkei, a majestic steppe of white stone mud building up against the carved out shoreline. Legend has it that the blue-white clay is naturally rejuvenating and visitors come to slather themselves with the self-generating mud, bake in the sun and then rinse and shed ten years off in the salty sea.

44  It was all she could do to not raise her arms in despair and frustration; she just wanted to read that goddamn book she'd been carrying around with her forever…

45  Persephone talking to herself—"not only was the cover of my book facing you upon your approach, but right, you walked all the way across the beach to ask me what book I was reading, god what happened to creativity. Or can't we just be past that anyhow, and

replied, "The Swan's Way, by Proust."[46] "By who?" "Proust." "Oh, yes of course, that's a classic."[47] "Yes, and I've just never read it and so this summer I decided I would finally read it." She followed up remarking how she's just been so busy that it has been hard to find the time to get through it, hoping he would catch on, but he didn't as yet. He carried on and talked about the latest book he'd just finished with a slight apology, it was a business book on entrepreneurship and a Portuguese language learning book. He'd been laid-off work almost a year now, and decided it was time to make more of a drastic change as it seemed clear he would not be finding new work in Sicily or on the mainland, and then joked that he'd most likely not find work anywhere in the Mediterranean.[48] Persephone acknowledged that she'd heard the Brazilian economy was expanding exponentially. He concurred and followed up with his love of the country and its people; he'd gone there on business a few years ago and fell in love and has gone back every year since. As would be expected the conversation rotated to Persephone and Persephone's future.

just be straight? Though I suppose that would be boring. If I were actually interested in the person then I probably wouldn't mind the obviousness of it, or at least not be frustrated by it." All this she reasoned to herself extremely quickly before responding.

46 She immediately felt embarrassed after saying that out loud.

47 Now she felt slightly more embarrassed.

48 This confession still wouldn't allow Persephone to let down her guard; she'd still left her job to pursue her ambitions. Though the confession did slightly raise her anxiety level.

"I'm an artist." She almost wanted to take it back the moment it left her lips, but it was too late. "Do you paint?"[49] "No, I'm a writer." Now she really felt anxious, as well she was starting to get frustrated as the time was getting on and she only had a half hour left before she had to pick up Maria and Juno at the station. "And what do you write? Do you do journalism or non-fiction, or do you write fiction?" She paused, "I used to write more non-fiction work, but now I'm working on fiction." He paused, "Oh, I see. So you're working on feeding your ego."[50] There was a long pause, perhaps even a pregnant pause or was it now actually impotent? Persephone was a bit beside herself, and replied, in a slightly less confident tone and manner of pronunciation, "umm, well yes, I guess that is what I'm doing—I'm in the business of feeding my ego."

She acknowledged the rock of clay in her hands that she'd reached over for earlier to 'genuinely' use as a scapegoat with the aim of deflecting a longer interlude with this "guy." He in turn was already in the midst of dismissing himself and rather sincerely, it appeared, said he enjoyed

49  "Why is painting always the default?" She knew "why" primarily, if she really wanted to spend the moment: once the notion of an artist was established, or re-established, in the Renaissance as being a master of humanities it became further broken down in the subsequent centuries with painting being considered its highest form of expression.
50  "What?" It was like a cut, like the director just said, "cut."

their conversation and wished her well. Persephone watched him walk away then stared out to sea. She was really somewhat dumbfounded, and the more she lingered there the more she wanted to thank him, to thank him for making a cut, for creating or causing a pause into her 'zone of freedom' in which she so fiendishly, and naïvely, thought she was setting out to be in the business of feeding an-other—a pedestrian—and then yes, herself.[51]

Unawares of her own movements, she moved towards the water and bent over with the chunk of clay she'd been coveting since earlier that afternoon and began to lather herself up until she had completely masked herself in the acclaimed white-blue clay. And stood still. Though, as it turns out, she had been pulled out to sea. And she hoped to remain there, out of time, as long as she could, if only that were (to be) a brief moment in time.

51 And certainly it was not lost on her a parallel claim that he too was in the business of serving his own (entrepreneurial) ego, and as well in making the trip across the beach to talk to her, perhaps he was also hoping to feed and service his libido. But that aside (and the non-revelatory case that artists are nothing but narcissistic, selfish, masturbatory, myopic etc.), she was affected; the comment still maintained its power and presence—it made the cut.

It's too flat to see the tomorrow
No no. Not

The endless view
never sees the horizon

It's always coming to go,
gone before it comes.

(sorry that seems so obvious)

but there's always the dust
that spreads as far

and, no it won't be found
perhaps recovered,

Cut.


persephone

*in-between places*

It was the second meeting of the Student's Federation for Thai Education Reformation or Revolution. "Revolution… or Reformation, as you like,"[1] is actually what the young high school student, Globe,[2] said to Styrene.[3]

1  Given the distance between the two options, "Revolution" and "Reformation," it struck Styrene rather curious the not so slight chasm between the two—'overthrow' or 'calibrate'—maybe its a marketing choice in the end.
2  To what degree she thought to make this name significant, or ironic (even if irony seemed appropriate), was unsure, though, for all intensive purposes, the name "Globe" was surely brilliant.
3  Speaking of names, Styrene had an uncomfortable relationship with her name. She'd had to grow into it, at least that's what she'd say. The name had always felt like an appendage, something stuck onto her though not of herself, but rather something that she had to take with, carry with her, always, along the way to be discerned, for. She'd often thought that it might have something to do with this one memory she had of her mother in what was presumably an attempt of endearment: this one morning her mother'd set to melody the phrase, "they called her styrene," and sang it while looking at her over a barely steaming cup of coffee. Yet the look never quite came into contact with endearment; the memory was always recalled as if there'd been a road-block between the gesture and its endearment; as though Styrene's mother had simply come across her lying on the side of the road and as she reached down to pick her up and examine her, a couple of road side workers having a lunch break in the tall, straw grasses adjacent to the road called out: "they called her Styrene."

Globe was one of about twenty kids who showed up for the meeting at the Reading Room, an archive and lending library dedicated to contemporary art and theory, where Styrene was slowly becoming the day's fixture and main user having arrived the moment it opened. It was her last day in Bangkok and she'd not yet made it to the Reading Room, although it was on her list of places, and so she was making up for lost time.[4] She'd been in Bangkok for six months, having left just once to Singapore in order to renew her visa. There was no particular reason she'd chosen to spend time in Bangkok other than the fact that it was cheap and she'd never been to Asia. And, she was, effectually, in between things, or places, as you like.[5]

4  Although that's actually rather questionable given that the majority of time Styrene had been in Bangkok she spent it online, as she was currently doing, just in another place—the Reading Room. There was really no making up time what so ever. Styrene forgot about time, all the time, until she'd feel behind.

5  "In-between places," citing the title… already, and so obviously, so situationally? For now, at least, yes. And to take advantage of this note, Styrene had read, or maybe even written, about the ever expanding and changing notion of place, where place as a concept, operates both geographically, as in "a place," and socially, signifying "one's place" as an aspect of identity. Yet, it was the author's contention, back at the turn of the century, that in an increasingly nomadic culture a sense of place becomes elusive. The emergence of globalism, and the subsequent capitalization of and on it, is shifting the boundaries of identity and geography, and as a result, place becomes valuable only as abstract nostalgia, or its value is superceded by what Paul Virilio calls the "strategic value of speed's 'noplace.'" Thus, she was "in-between places" or perhaps we may not even need a noun and could just say that she was in between.

Foyfon Chaimongkol, 2013, charcoal on paper, courtesy of the artist

Globe and company were full of enthusiasm, anxious to get started on their revolution of the education system, emphasizing the demand that "education must begin with students" as that is where it "ends up."[6] Their first meeting apparently took place about a month ago and was less a meeting and more a disparate accumulation of adolescence and their convictions in the backroom of a, mostly, inhabitable storefront out in Bangkapi (about an hour from city center). Now, through the generosity of the Reading Room director, they took up their meetings in the alternative space centrally located in the Silom district of Bangkok, ironically one of the most important financial districts in the city.[7]

6  https://www.facebook.com/Thailandstudentmovement

Meanwhile, Styrene was still working on upgrading her avatar; she'd become bored already with Judith, her character, and subsequent characteristics, now all seemingly commonplace. At first,[8] Styrene was taken with Judith—she'd always longed to have an avatar, would joke about it often in fact, amongst friends though she was absolutely serious in wanting an avatar to represent herself.[9] She'd actually spent an enormous amount of time generating "Judith" even though she barely employed the avatar to its full capacity. Still it was Judith who was essentially now her sole arbiter online, through whom Styrene operated, and navigated, online. Judith had her own email, filled out

7   But is it ironic, actually? Simply because alternative and financial have been traditionally exclusive of each other? Really? "Nowadays" haven't such situational situations become institutionally discrete, and distinct, coextensively? Thus, eschewing over-performing irony.

8  As is most often the case with all things.

9  Which, as one of her more politically active friends would like to emphasize, was perhaps, not so much different from having an elected politician represent oneself, something about which many people are absolutely serious and—as opposed to Styrene—would not often joke about. To this Styrene would typically role her eyes, not simply at the obviousness of the analogy, or obvious stretch of the analogy, but as well as to emphasize her friend's insistence on reducing everything to politics, which is not to say there wasn't truth in the analogy—it is a politics of representation "perhaps" at all levels. Yet she'd hoped, or only hoped in response, for a place outside of, or maybe just alongside, the "political" in which representation wasn't so encumbered. Is that an in-between place or is this just a convenient place to reassert this story's title? Regardless, in the fantasy of the avatar is the fantasy of appearing rather than representing. Perhaps it was a "zone of freedom" that was fantasized in the avatar, all of which she knew would be rendered, variably, obsolete once the avatar came into existence, and employment, or, losing all hope, was always already *a priori* anyhow. And so, yes, perhaps it was all politics—that appearing, or simply showing up, had become representation already—a politics of representation, representing one self as one's representational self. And, yet, aside from this mounting discourse in and outside of her head and her politics, she'd really just wanted someone to show-up, unencumbered in her place (perhaps, precisely so that she could 'simply' be appearing).

forms, purchased goods, employed Pay Pal, etc. Thus, Styrene intended to take it seriously,[10] even if only in name, and having read up on avatar generation she was now convinced of its strident signification.[11] In one memorable passage she recalled the shared sense of import:

> *Choosing an avatar is one of the most important actions a person takes when embarking on any sort of an online life. Your avatar becomes your visual representation on the interwebs; it is the only visual representation many of your online friends will ever have of you.[12]*

The whole avatar obsession was somehow related to her "job" in which she'd developed an online relationship with a Gold Farmer. Her brother was a slightly obsessed *World of Warcraft* player (and he's not alone as it's the largest subscribing multi-player online game). Overtime he'd become acquainted with a particular Gold Farmer and eventually befriended him. The guy had become the relentless target of abuse by

10  That's a complete lie.
11  Though really the excessive time spent on the avatar was due more to her (once more) being 'in-between places' and it was simply a way to help divert attention away from being in a particular place. As well, it was essentially a result of her "work," therefore, as an act of utility it justified the obsession.
12  The emphasis on the visual didn't discount her feigned sense of import she relegated to her avatar status as Styrene reminded herself that there was a face, so-to-speak, behind the representation.

various gamers and while Davide, Styrene's brother, didn't approve of gold farming he sympathized with the Gold Farmers, and moreover, was utterly amazed by the existence, ingenuity and success of such a shadow, virtually produced, economy.

"Gold Farming is a 'literal-virtuality,'" as Davide like to say, "a Gold Farmer farms for gold, in the virtual world of a game." Styrene thought he was joking when she'd first heard this, but she could tell by her brother's tone and enthusiasm that he was completely serious, not to mention enthralled. While Davide's sister had no patience for her brother's detailed accounts of the "World of Warcraft" she was mildly interested in this notion of a "gold farmer" more generally, especially in its existence in a virtual world, which took her a while to fully believe.

As Davide had explained, "Gold Farmers play the game for money, it's a job. If you play for a long time and typically hang-out in one area 'farming mobs,' which means killing entities (like a monster), that reap rewards, such as game money, like gold coins, or powerful items that can be used for advancement in the game." "So, they're game fanatics too," Styrene said rather dismissively. "Maybe they are too, but don't forget we're talking about roughly 20 million 'fanatics' here Styrene and it's generated an enormous alternative economy, some say up to 7 billion now!" She was impressed by the numbers, but still seemed to think it was fanatically ridiculous, and, perhaps in part for a sibling slight, she followed in tone, "you mean an enormous 'virtual' alternative economy, right?" "Not exactly Styrene, so lose the attitude. The 'gold' or assets, etc. are 'farmed' in the game, so yes, in the virtual world of the game, but it is then sold for REAL money in the REAL world to REAL people." Davide was getting annoyed. "That's insane!" Davide was now annoyed. "It's not anymore insane than people buying shit because it makes them feel better. The practicality of the situation is that a lot of people don't have the time outside of work to play the game enough to further build up their assets and so they buy them, which allows them more access, and presumably more fun in the game."[13] "I see," said Styrene.

*   *   *

The Gold Farmer's English was rudimentary at best, which was a primary reason he'd end up the recipient of repeated attacks, coupled with his repetitive gaming gestures, as he was presumed, as many non-English speaking players are, and in this case accurately, Chinese and hence a Gold Farmer given China is home to the largest number of Gold Farming operations. Somehow, over time, Davide was able to develop a rapport with the Gold Farmer, as he tended to watch out for him in *World of Warcraft*. This, their rapport, had taken quite a while to develop, as Styrene would come to learn, in part because Gold Farmers

13 Now she really wanted to freak out and go off on a diatribe, regardless of how obvious it would be, which it was, on how this was just the most 'obvious' example of a deteriorating society. 'Of course,' she thought 'even in the virtual world of games, one can just buy their way in, and out, and about! Buy access. Buy fun.' We could put the rest of the diatribe in this note, but it'd just be taking up space—you can fill in the blanks. Davide probably did, in Styrene's stifling.

are instructed not to be social. "No Chatting, No Downloading, No Socializing," are the general Gold Farmers' employee rules, along with strategic ones, such as: memorize the game maps; scout around quickly to find a good, unpopulated area; don't move around too much; stay in the same place and kill the same 'monster' over and over again; if any other players come, do not engage just fight them off and don't give up your place; accumulate as much 'gold' as possible.

Styrene could easily piece together how such mandated behavior would easily generate a quasi-trademark of the typical Gold Farmer, and hence 'give them away'. According to Davide, the whole Gold Farming phenomena had become a big deal, and industry, causing all sorts of issues inside, and perhaps outside, the gaming world. Now she could understand, or believe, Davide's stories about organized gangs that had developed with the sole purpose of killing off Gold Farmers— supposedly, "growing to a population of close to a million!" Davide exclaimed. And would continue to elaborate on the riff between hard-core gamers, Gold Farmers and those in-between. Davide saw himself as part of the latter and could sympathize with the gamers who claimed it simply wasn't fair play, and the Gold Farmer's who simply needed a job. He also saw it as an evolutionary development—one that amazed him and in large part kept him in the game. Davide didn't have enough time to play the game incessantly, building up assets that would gain him greater access and ability, and hence to take advantage of the vast developments in game play. Therefore he would often purchase items and/or money from game Brokers. For hard-core gamers, this was considered blasphemy Davide told Styrene, "because they don't think it's fair to buy rather than earn, and they say it artificially upsets the game economy."[14]

14 This morsel almost sent Styrene spinning out of control in what she coined an "inane logic of contradiction." And of course, she was thinking the obvious again in this analogy or evidence of the deterioration of society through these accountings of "the worlds of warcraft" by Davide. Sure she thought, 'people get pissed because assets become disproportionately available yet those same gamers who decry the inequality that arises from gold farming don't account for the possibility of their own disproportionate circumstances!' She was kind-of getting irate, in her head, as the argument seemed based on the simplicity of the idea of 'playing by the rules'. Styrene, in obvious Leftist fashion, began to question the economies of the various players were the circumstances in which they played the game fair? Might some players have various and varying advantages due to availability of time, financial stability for game subscriptions, quality and capability of the machines on which they played... She could have gone on, and into a whole added diatribe about class, culture, and access in the real world that too could be critiqued if the sole issue were one of *fairness*. But she stopped—she was bored, and feeling resigned already. Sure, she thought, Gold Farming isn't necessarily legal in game regulation so that makes the argument 'cut and dry' while the other argument is, as it is in any world, nebulous and varying in visibility. Regardless, she thought it was kind of brilliant and ingenious, and clearly was proving more beneficial to the overall game economy than detrimental—it exists, quite successfully. Then she wondered if this 'determined accident' would qualify, and quantify, as a good 'accelerationist' model—it was worth pondering at least.

It was in fact one of the 'Destroy All Gold Farmers' gangs that had gone after 'Davide's Gold Farmer,' and, consequently, what essentially brought them together. Perhaps it was something out of ignorance that they banded together as there was a growing sense of fundamentalism in the anti-gold farming groups. Davide had noticed 'his' Gold Farmer in the same spot he'd seen him the day before. He remembered it vividly because "it was like it'd been planned in my reality; 'Attack of the Chiggers,' had just landed on my playlist, then at the same time these guys came from all corners to attack and ambush this Gold Farmer. It was totally random, and kind of hilarious. Then, and I'm not even sure why I did it except that these hard-core self-imposed game governors just pissed me off and the whole in-game ambush seemed kind of psycho, so I just called them off and said I was teaching him how to play the game, or something like that. Mainly I got them to think he was somehow 'my' guy and he/we weren't Gold Farmers. They didn't believe me at first, but I threatened to file complaints with one of the GMs [Game Masters] and they backed off."[15] "The Gold Farmer still wouldn't talk to me for a

15 Styrene was again feeling overwhelmed with despair with these game reports—why is such energy, such collective organizing and action taking place inside a virtual game space? Why couldn't such energy be put into practice in the real world? And surely, Styrene wasn't the first person to ask this question—she'd just remembered a woman from a TED talk she'd watched a few years ago that focused on harnessing 'this gamer power to solve real-world problems.' Of course she had to look it up again, while she was supposedly intently listening to Davide's recounting via Skype. It was Jane McGonigal, the gamer developer who'd overcome a traumatic concussion through developing a collective 'wellness' game and whose goal it was for the next decade "to try to make it as easy to save the world in real life as it is to save the world in online games." "Well, at least someone's got that covered," Styrene thought, and "what a place to work, *Institute for the Future*," then, after inquiring about employment opportunities, somehow, she felt more despair—for Styrene it was all just very *speculative*, and that word somehow abused her.

bit, probably because he wasn't sure if I was 'under-cover' or not, and more, as I found out, because his English wasn't very good. Though he did manage to say, 'thank you,' and 'are you stupid?' pretty good, huh!"

* * *

And so, it was through this slightly bizarre and precarious rendering of 'trust' that Davide came to know the Gold Farmer, and came to offer him a proposition: online English lessons in return for in-game currency. And for Davide this meant he'd farm out the English lessons to his sister, Styrene, who could, presumably, actually teach English. In total it took Davide three and a half Skype "meetings" for her to be convinced of its value or rather her value asset in a virtual attempt to teach language.[16]

And what she hadn't yet discovered was that actually, 'good gaming' or 'serious games' had a history and had spawned an entire industry itself though not one that necessarily merged with, or co-mingled with games and gamers the likes of *World of Warcraft*.

16 And she still wasn't convinced of the value, in the online world. Sure, she could understand the desire and demand, and its subsequent alternative market effect, but rationalize it, no. And yet, the awareness of her rationalized complicity in accepting the "job" only had the effect of annoying her, causing merely caution rather than hindrance in taking it on—she needed cash. And she realized that she could further rationalize the situation such that providing instruction in the English language could amount to a value of mobility whether in the virtual realm or the real one for the Gold Farmer, and this thinking further afforded Styrene with a sense of value—purpose.

The set-up was as such: Davide would pay Styrene an hourly wage to develop and implement English lessons; this wage would accumulate in immaterial value to be used as 'barter,' or currency, in order to exchange, or buy, immaterial game objects and/or game currency; the Gold Farmer delivers the game objects or currency to Davide as payment for English lessons received from Styrene. It was all rather simple and easy in Davide's mind, and perhaps in all their minds, yet as Styrene would come to understand, entrepreneurial Gold Farming wasn't so easy.

Unlike Styrene, the Gold Farmer couldn't merely develop game assets at his leisure and betroth them at his will. He couldn't simply sell gaming assets while generating them at work. The Gold Farmer and his co-workers were closely supervised and any asset was effectually inventoried, to be sold by the boss to a broker. It was not then, necessarily, possible for them to generate 'gold' while working and sell it on their own, on their own black market; they were employees of a very, albeit immaterial, controlled and monitored black market. Therefore, the Gold Farmer had to moonlight for English lessons, which after ten to twelve hours of on the job gaming already would only afford him six to eight hours at best outside the game. Again, this wasn't easy either as his only computer was the one at work, which was, along with his avatar, immediately picked up by his tandem co-worker to keep the character in-play, and generating assets, 24/7.

Fortunately, the Gold Farmer managed to find a small cybercafé nearby where he could play for Davide. It was close enough to get to rather quickly from his place of work, which was also his place of rest, although far enough away from it that he could be sure he wouldn't run into his boss or co-workers. Davide decided to maintain his *World of Warcraft* account and share it with the Gold Farmer; they both could play the same account and that way all the assets the Gold Farmer generated for Davide would already be 'assumed' for Davide in the game thus avoiding the registration of any actual transactions. Of course there was the chance that the Gold Farmer could steal Davide's account and/or all its assets yet he wasn't a dealer, and if he started dealing with Brokers word would probably get around in the small underground network in Jinhua where he was based—and not everything plays out virtually. There was also the chance the account could get banned if the *World of Warcraft* parent company caught on, but the Gold Farmer assured Davide his IP address would be masked and that he'd stick to the moderately progressive and fluctuating gaming schedule Davide had devised to get started. So, for Davide, and presumably the Gold Farmer, the apparatus was in place, and so was their unspoken trust, now he just needed Styrene, or Judith, to situate herself in the game.

*   *   *

Davide introduced Styrene cum Judith to the Gold Farmer via new email accounts he'd set-up for each of them specifically for this exchange and its subsequent transactions. They would also employ Skype and TOMonline, for conversing and working on pronunciation (plus it was good to have dual modes of communication given the possibility of communication blocking in China). It was at this time that Styrene decided to generate an avatar.[17] As part of her willingness to work with and for her brother, he agreed to make manifest its image and thus Judith was born in homage to Styrene's favorite painting.

Caravaggio, *Judith Beheading Holofernes*, 1598-99, Oil on Canvas, Galleria Nazionale d'Arte Antica, Palazzo Barberini Rome

17  It was actually her brother's idea, all along as a pre-caution, but at first Styrene thought he was just getting carried away in day dreaming about the possibilities of being tracked as though they were embarking on an espionage scheme. (It's also at this time that we could easily turn this whole narrative into a cynical quasi-action sci-fi flick—a low-budget, B-movie style flick—crossing in and between *Bourne Identity, Fight Club, Gamer* and the in-production movie, *Warcraft*). And again, since we're here in this note

Judith proceeded to develop lesson plans as well as compile tutorial and translation links for the Gold Farmer alongside her own quasi-developmental stages, as Judith. At first Judith operated mostly as an image for the two to interface through to transmit English language learning exercises. She was essentially like a storefront or a display case through which to disseminate and accept information.[18] Yet over time they developed together as Judith, or developed "Judith" together, as Judith was the only character the Gold Farmer interacted with in English (outside the nominal exchanges with Davide about game play and the discriminating rants in *World of Warcraft*). All of his English exercises, trials, errors, accomplishments, thoughts, responses and soon conversations, were taken up with Judith, thus Judith became "Judith" through a quasi "call and response" mechanism required in language, as in the most basic language learning beginnings.

perhaps it's worth noting that it took Styrene at least a few weeks to ease into calling what she referred to as her online-alter-ego an "avatar." It felt awkward, and ridiculous, like she was masquerading in a place, and a name, she didn't belong. It wasn't until the idea of "avatar" became more of an object of mobility—a staging apparatus she could set in motion that could or would take on a (virtual) life of its own in being alter to her, an apparatus that could become a staging ground upon and with which she alternates not simply actions, but ideas, her ideas—that she could carry it.

18  Sure, one could absolutely employ the "hologram" metaphor, though it seems too obvious and perhaps it was the setting of Bangkok that immediately, almost imminently, conjured the idea of a vendor, as well as its relation to exchange, which is closer to what was taking place overall.

*Where are you from?*

> *China.*

*[Shit, no, I mean] What is the name of the town you were born?*
> *Hangzhou.*

*You can also say, "I was born in Hangzhou."*
*Practice with complete sentence.*
> *Ok.*

*Where do you live?*

> *Jinhua.*

*Ok. You can say, "I live in Jinhua." What is your profession?*
> *No profession.*

*What is your job?*

> *Gamer. I play World of*
> *Warcraft for my job.*

*Do you have any siblings?*

> *What sibling?*

*[Is "sibling" not in the translator? Shit, well maybe not so commonly*
*used, is it?] Do you have any brothers? Do you have any sisters?*
> *One brother.*

*Does your brother work with you?*
> *No. He is home.*

*What did you do today?*

> *Today I played World of*

*Warcraft. All day and night.*

*What do you like to do in your free time?*
*No free time.*

*You never have free time?*
*Sometimes I play music.*

*Are you a musician?*
*Sometimes. More I am gamer. Do you free time? And what?*

*[Ummm. I guess I'm supposed to answer. To have exchange. It's been a few weeks or so, and I'm mainly just a vending machine of questions to be answered. What would Judith say?] Sometimes. I read or travel.*
*I cannot travel.*

*I understand. Mostly, I "travel" in my city.*
*Ok.*
*Do you have job?*

*Yes. I teach English.*
*Like me?*

*[Shit. I guess it wouldn't be a good idea to tell him that he is my only student. Would he understand, in language, that Judith is teaching English only to support her project to creatively repurpose sites as/ for/with collective community exchange locally based within an international network? Is that really Judith's future anyway? And how can she explain that in basic English?] Yes. And I make art.*

*You are artist.*

*[Sure.] Yes.*
*Do you have a dream?*

*I want music for my job.*
*And play games for fun.*

*[Judith wants to play language for fun and make collectivity her job*
*along with Styrene.]*

As the language skills develop so too do the conversational features and content—language is the apparatus—thus for Styrene, and Judith, the "job" became more about the genesis of identities and possibilities in an alternate space straddling fiction than it was about teaching the English language.[19]

\* \* \*

Styrene couldn't help but be distracted by the student gathering, the youngest of whom was maybe thirteen, the oldest seventeen. She was

---

19 Judith surmised that she was similar to an economy of language—the avatar is a stand-in, or more radically a stand*ing* towards—as in the words of Jane McGonigal, the woman of the Future Institute, "Avatars are a way to express our true selves, our most heroic, idealized version of who we might become." Yet how is it that 'avatar' became bound to a politics of representation that is already inscribed? Circumscription makes the menu; and so who's writing one's future fiction? Judith had Styrene cornered, and it was uncomfortable—surely teaching English would've been easier.

sure that she'd been at least twenty-seven before she attempted to take education seriously and perhaps another five years before she thought of it, or became aware of education as a self-advocating right. Here though, were students, too young to vote, flopped on baby blue bean bag chairs, oversized charcoal grey pillows, and seat cushions gathered in a quasi nuclei cluster of determination in the corner of the room in this narrow 4th floor walk-up, committed to advocating their right to representation.

Three of them, adolescent boys, were strewn across a long narrow burgundy davenport[20] underneath a bank of windows that framed, along with fore grounded trees, a stylistically architectural 'conglomerate' with two adorning torch-bearing figurative sculptures atop the building's name calling out "Best Thai" in a font variation close to that of *Times New Roman*. Set further back stood a sterile office building for AIA, a life insurance company.[21] Seated in the middle of the three was Netiwit, the master of ceremony; agile and at the ready he sat on the edge of the sofa cushion and leaned forward with the conviction and forthrightness

20 "Davenport" was the word her grandmother used to refer to what Styrene always regarded as a "sofa," regardless of whether or not the 'sofa' encumbered a place to sleep. In this case, Styrene employed the term properly and was not only pleased with the accurate employment of the term, but as well with the possibility of sleep if it came to be.
21 Incidentally, Styrene had read that morning in *The Nation*, one of Bangkok's English-language newspapers, that "Ordinary life insurance witnessed the highest growth compared with other types at Bt329.665 billion, up 17.90 per cent. Whole life insurance enjoyed the highest market share of 48.34 per cent among all ordinary life insurance types." Perhaps there was a formidable reason or at least utility to the consumption of stated market update—wholeness. Somehow this put things in context (or maybe just the view) at least situationally, and temporally.

of any aspiring leader. He was wearing a black t-shirt advocating the adjudication of article 112, *lèse-majesté*, the long-standing law that deems it a crime to speak or act out against sovereign rule, and as well, here, the royal family. As of late, it was explained, the pre-exisiting law was being exploited by Royalists to ensure and fortify their power within a society increasingly expanding its bounds. To someone like Styrene, Netiwit's t-shirt was simply a series of numbers, more or less innocuous, in white and yellow. Yet of course, the t-shirt, produced by "Same Sky," a leftist publishing group whose regular magazine was often censored and banned, represented a radical charge. Styrene, anticipating a level of meaning more than innocuous, wrote down the sequence:

1 1 2

20:00

7 8 9

The first sequence could now be understood as representing Article 112, *lèse-majesté,* yet the second numeral "1" was rendered in yellow, as were the numbers "7" and "9"; the rest were in white. "20:00" referred to the time of day that the Royal News is broadcasted on television. The numerals "7," "8" and "9" represent the Rama Kings, VII, VIII and IX, the latter of whom is incumbent. While the reigning King's effectual power is limited within the contemporary institution, his authorial influence and respect is ideally indisputable. His number is in yellow, which while suggesting the Royal Family color, it also highlights him in association with the numeral one of the first stanza, and the seventh of the Rama Kings. The yellow numeral one, the central highlighted number of

Article 112, also represents Rama I, in this coded construction, and thus, the controversially held opinion that they [Rama I, VII, IX] maintain(ed) anti-democratic positions.

Netiwit, the bearer of the 'code,' came to find his place, and position, in his questioning of the strict, and strictly enforced, Thai Hair Regulations for Students (crew cuts for young boys and short bobs for young girls, slightly longer for secondary school). Within the writing of the formal complaint a "manifesto" of sorts developed, and was later posted on an online student site to gain support, to claim its case and justify its claim:[22]

> *The hair regulation is contrary to the Thai constitution …*
>
> *The military-style rule for school children is unnecessary and instills in children harmful authoritarian values …*
>
> *[It] makes youth not learn how to think … only follow orders, …*
>
> *[It] promotes abuse of power by teachers and teaches youth to absorb such irrational power abuse …*
>
> *[It] gives rise to insults on human dignity [verbal abuse by teachers given as an example]…*

22  Thanks to Coy, the director of the Reading Room, not only did she allow Styrene to make herself at home at the Reading Room, she helped to translate and provided her with helpful information, (such as an updated overview and English translation of the various statements, complaints and regulatory laws: http://asiancorrespondent. com/95321/thailand-whats-hair-got-to-do-with-childrens-rights/).

What began as a singular complaint, filed with the NHRC, has spawned a much larger "movement" in which the opposition to student hair regulation, while a pertinent and real issue in and of itself, has also become a stand-in for the over-arching issues embedded—authoritarian control, censorship, freedom of expression, hierarchy, repression/suppression, etc. The "hair revolution" is now a "student revolution" that seeks to abolish all existing hair regulations for students en route to wide-spread education reform, spearheaded by the young Netiwit.

Now, somewhat an activist figure of notoriety he was at the center, or as Styrene surmised, the epicenter of the birth of a movement, or revolution, depending. He'd taken to the role like a seasoned counsel beginning the meeting with a historical overview of absolute monarchy, a discussion on the dominance and rule of elitist clans and the development and power relations of, and among, nation states.[23]

22 Thanks to Coy, the director of the Reading Room, not only did she allow Styrene to make herself at home at the Reading Room, she helped to translate and provided her with helpful information, (such as an updated overview and English translation of the various statements, complaints and regulatory laws: http://asiancorrespondent. com/95321/thailand-whats-hair-got-to-do-with-childrens-rights/).

23 Styrene tried not to feel as small as she was feeling but it was too late; Judith took over. And she began to think of herself in the size of Judith, her avatar, which she held to be small. In essence this could very well be inaccurate, in terms of scale at least: governed by a sequence of numbers with more or less functionality, it's immaterial, and scale becomes more or less immeasurable. Thus, regardless of how the numbers add up, regardless of the code, size had no place, literally and metaphorically. It was now all pure functionality, Judith attempted to argue, functional meaning.

While she continued in earnest to pick up bits and pieces of an abbreviated translation of the proceedings between the director and a recent visitor to the space ("probably European" Styrene thought), the blue covered Gramsci book came into view. It topped a stack of books in the middle of the table where she'd taken up residence. Peering over her computer screen to catch the title, she then noticed Chomsky's *Occupy* text, which ends with advice for the Occupy protesters in the U.S. from the National Lawyers Guild.[24] It was poignantly occupying a position atop another stack of books between her screen and Gramsci's place—surely this was the setting of a scene. With more or less to occupy, as yet, here this group of kids were occupying a room, though more importantly a moment, that of their genesis, in their legitimizing their coming together as a collective organization replete with the assigning and naming of principals and roles—becoming "official."

\* \* \*

## THE MOMENT ART CHANGED FOREVER

There was a 2008 poster from the Tate Modern that proclaimed "THE MOMENT ART CHANGED FOREVER"[25] underneath a Dada-esque

---

24 It was published as a "Penguin Special" she'd noticed, produced by what's become known as "Zuccotti Park Press" and the "Occupied Media Pamphlet Series." She'd skipped to the end where the pamphlet series ended with a quote from their "forthcoming pamphlet" by Angela Davis, "We transform the meaning of occupation. We turn occupation into something that is beautiful, something that brings community together, something that calls for love and happiness and hope." Styrene sighed, in awe and despair.
25 And in that moment of reading Styrene had a salient desire to have had that moment too, yet of course how often is it that those moments are only moments after the moment

stylistic attempt at 'fonting' the names "Duchamp, ManRay, Picabia"[26] and (surprise surprise!) slightly above and across the inevitable urinal. It reminded her of the moment in which through a strict economy of language means she'd attempted to explain contemporary art to the Gold Farmer. It was during a moment in which she'd no longer wanted to operate as Judith coming to know the Gold Farmer as such Styrene was feeling cumbersome in the sincerity he appeared to offer himself to Judith. Yet once the subtle nuances of Styrene's character started to proliferate, due to varying inevitable breaches of staying in character, communication necessarily began to fail. It was no longer a direct and determined message, but rather one too encoded with persuasion—Judith's persuasion. Here there was a protocol, English language instruction, and Judith was the interface through which it streamed, and deviation wasn't part of the code though it filled the space in between.

Thus it was hard not to be nostalgic about putting Judith to rest as it had occupied her everyday over the past six months, but more importantly

has passed such that there's no knowing, as such, in such moments. Would there be another "the moment art changed forever?" Or is it that aesthetics is now so indelibly inclusive of the conceptual, which can account for everything and nothing, that there is no "moments" left. Right, and this line of thinking is simply a re-hashing of post 60s 'death of avant-garde' ideology, which she knew, which she knew everyone knew, already. Still, she liked the sound, or maybe the saying of, "the moment art changed forever," both for its profound facticity and its factitious ambition.

26 Styrene wondered how often her surroundings simply told her story, navigated her route, piecing it together like the seemingly random bits of a puzzle (this puzzle bit is reminiscent of self-help vignettes she'd read, in which she was convinced that the pieces of her puzzle of life, in the desperate metaphor, were surely from different puzzles entirely that had coalesced into a dysfunctional shuffled collection culminated from a vast array of second-hand stores, yard sales, unwanted gifts, dumpster finds and flea markets.

it is how she'd come to know Judith and the Gold Farmer. As Judith she learned that the Gold Farmer worked (played *World of Warcraft*) 10-12 hours a day for his boss and then a few more hours for his English lessons; that in his 'spare' time[27] he played in what he deemed a "White Metal Band" called *Toxic Beach*, slept or practiced Buddhist meditation, in secret; that he made grassy field plant arrangements from clippings he'd scrabble together on his walks home from the cybercafé for his mother, which he couldn't mail, but would photograph with his mobile phone; that he lost his father when he was ten; that he'd longed to be in the opera (which he'd only heard from sitting in the school master's office in detention), yet his father had discouraged such an outrageous promotion not least due to their class; that he'd started playing video games on one of three rental computers at the convenience shop when he was eight in exchange for re-stocking the shelves, but he never wanted it to be a "profession." It was such rendering of a person, of twenty-two years, that Styrene understood Judith's futility as her asset, as nothing more than a vector graphic born of causality to which she only became a tangential entity in her utility.

*　*　*

---

27  It was beyond Judith's comprehension when this "spare time" actually occurred as she could never calculate it actually existing. She would often get caught up doing the numbers and lost in the possibility that there was another sense of time virtually. She'd even once asked him if he played in a real band or played in a virtual band—the Gold Farmer was obviously offended and confused. She let it stand, and decided to accept that his band played on his few days off a month—somewhere.

The guy who'd been sitting next to her, Zoyd, claimed to be from Sorkino, a village in the Russian Saratov region and considered one of Russia's foremost kazoo virtuosos. He was in Bangkok to teach Stalinist Studies at one of the elite private university's specializing in Business & Economics degrees. All this he presented voluntarily as he'd wanted to engage with Styrene and even thought to "spontaneously" play a tune on his kazoo (he always carries one in his coat pocket), yet he soon recalled it was a reading room. Perhaps, in seeing the rather curious look on Styrene's face, he attempted to say more, fill the gap, "I guess its not every day you meet a Stalinist specialist!"[28] And in fact it wasn't, it may have even been the first time. "I do have to admit that I pull a larger audience for my kazoo then I do for my 'Structural Stalinism' classes." Styrene's face didn't change much, but she smiled and nodded having been taken at least with his thick and staccato sounding Russian accent.

Yet, Styrene chose to maintain close proximity with her computer screen so as to quietly say, "no thank you, I do not want to engage." This became partially clear to Zoyd and he meandered over to the only corner bookshelf in the room. He stood there for a while it seemed, perusing what was on offer, Styrene wasn't really paying attention, yet, due to the capability enabled through peripheral vision, she'd registered that he'd eventually pulled a book off the shelf and took a seat with it over in the corner. After a while she'd forgotten he was even there, the periphery

---

28   Completing the declaration, Styrene added (to herself), "in Bangkok" ; "in a progressive reading room in the middle of a capitalist financial center" ; "yes, its not everyday."

having given way to the interior, and she was more or less alone. Until he arrived again at the shared table and set down next to Styrene's 'place' a book. It was titled *In/Different Spaces: place and memory in visual culture* by Victor Burgin. Before taking his absolute leave, Zoyd leaned forward and whispered in Styrene's ear, "Victor Burgin understood images less in traditional terms of the specific institutions that produce them [...] and more as hybrid mental constructs composed of fragments derived from the heterogeneous sources that together constitute the 'media.'"[29]

With that in her head, it was as if everything was becoming a construct, fragments simply gathering in and around her contours and contrasts. Just as she was, mostly, settling into her new avatar, that was fittingly comprised of a montage of free floating images and projections. She started to toy with the idea of creating a Facebook page for him though before she typed H-O-L-O-F-E-R-N-E-S into the Facebook search field, a friend's post popped up just below in the news feed:[30]

29 It was a rather dramatic exit, surely, not to mention coyly intimate, unless of course it was simply all drama, then the "intimacy" becomes purely theatrical, though not dismissive, it's effects are there often heightened even if not wholly substantiated. Nonetheless, well said, or well surmised, she thought. Then she thought, or so we think she thought (Styrene's were often too cumulus to decipher), that perhaps this was the way in which the GMO protagonists thought in terms of their argumentation.
30 In case it's worth underscoring for an easy imbedded chide on Facebook, it was one of those friends whom Styrene had never met and actually really had no idea how it was they presumably knew each other (these moments caused her to wonder the effects of Facebook on the notion of six degrees of separation), but in this place it was a friend, perhaps a very, old, dear friend; perhaps a fictional friend.

"Have you ever walked away from what others had learned to expect and accept from you? It is so eternally satisfying. And only the true people will support you, mainly family, but if you can reach beyond that slight sliver of consciousness there may just be that one that will be there for the long run. That special one will pass the test and know the snakeskin left behind in the mutation from then to now is no longer you. They will cease to parade around the false you and instead accept the new but same you."

The statement caused Styrene pause, for various reasons not the least of which was Judith and her fate,[31] as well as her own. Though just as she was about to lapse into memory, both backwards and forwards, she was distracted once again, this time by the volume of a conversation seemingly revolving around meditation.[32] It was odd, or maybe it was merely coincidental, that the afternoon hour was becoming habited by the 'spiritual' as just earlier she'd overheard a young woman from Mexico City talking to the director about her volunteer work with the Peace Revolution, a global project sponsored by the Dhammakaya Temple. In short, the revolution's agenda is to promote meditation following the logic that if one finds inner peace within the self then peace will transmit

31 And she was getting a bit carried away, pondering the idea of writing a memoir on behalf of Judith—it would be entitled *The Memoir of Becoming Judith* chronicling her six months existence, which paralleled Styrene's six months in Bangkok the majority of which she spent in online places.
32 "Seemingly" because Styrene didn't really know what they were talking about, at least in terms of a direct translation as they were speaking in Thai. Yet by certain gestures and perhaps even the few words she learned, she garnered that the conversation was about meditation. One could also propose that the relics already of the day, including the recent Facebook post, were influencing her "translation."

through one's community, as well, with and through the practice of meditation. Styrene wondered, while overhearing the exchange, if such a simple formula was actually plausible, let alone believable, and yet perhaps it was the simplicity that befell us all.[33]

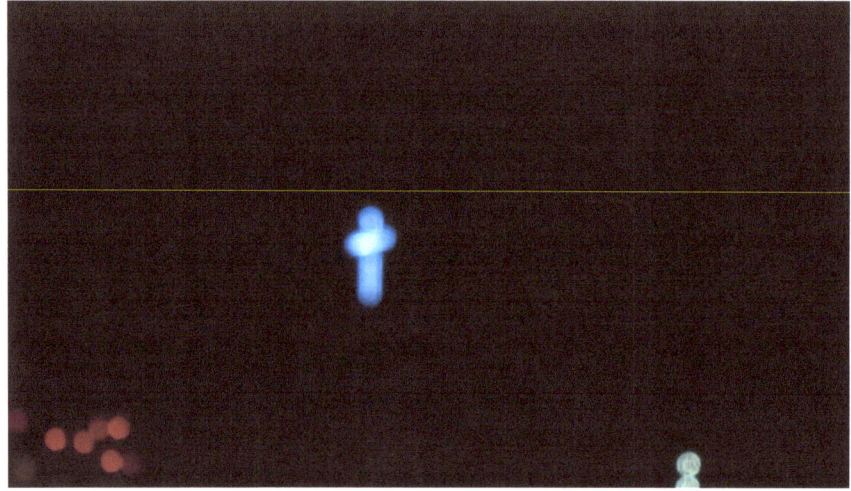

34

33 That's actually not true; Styrene had a much more cynical reaction: not for a moment, well maybe an instant, did she think such simplicity or even the notion of peace was at all plausible.

34 The image was detected and decided yet remained un-photographed; it was going to be replaced by one of the author's favorite works, *AC/DC* (1997) by Hills Snyder (hillssnyder.com), but then the wonderful Kyo shot the photo and sent it along.

Simplistic or not, Styrene ended up listening to the girl's story, and not simply because she appeared so convinced and convincing. Luz Maria was set to work with the Peace Revolution for six months translating the NGO's texts from English into Spanish, to facilitate their expanding market, as well as continuing her work as a "peace coach." She'd come to the peace revolution through their website ("*A high quality online interactive program to empower yourself through inner peace in 42 days*") through which she'd learned to meditate and in turn learn to coach others through the process of meditation, or more precisely *meditation for peace*. After coaching for about a year, online, she'd decided she wanted to pilgrimage to the epicenter of the peace revolution, which is located within the sprawling domain of the Dhammakaya Temple just outside of Bangkok. When questioned about her association with the Temple by Coy, the director of the Reading Room,[35] Luz Maria was sure to stress the secularism of the Peace Revolution—while it was a sponsored project of the Buddhist Temple one did not have to be or become a Buddhist to engage in the Buddhist based meditational practices or embrace the practice of peace through meditation.

---

35 After eavesdropping for a good portion of the day she'd finally figured out the director's name, or at least she thought she did. Regardless, it just felt nice for Styrene to assume her now by name, which over-rode the name's accuracy.

Coy was 'buying it' ("*For $100, we provide 1 medal of honor, 1 meditation CD and bumper stickers as gifts of gratitude*"), so it appeared. It also appeared as though she was trying to navigate the discussion as diplomatically, or perhaps just politely, as she could withstand as it also appeared as though Coy was stammering to divulge something about the Temple, generally speaking, and the Temple's standing in Thai society. Essentially, from what Styrene could glean between the pauses, the Dhammakaya Temple had a similar reputation to that of the Church of Scientology.[36] In some regards it actually appeared akin to the Catholic tradition as well in that one can allegedly purchase their level of Karma as needed, or afforded.

*  *  *

36 Being from the United States that was Styrene's immediate, appropriately or inappropriately, association. Further, it was Styrene's contention, in the span of this twenty minute exchange she was privy to, that perhaps there was in fact something to the whole UFO thing, at least as form given the Dhammakaya Temple architecture encouraged that form (perhaps another parallel with sci-fi writer L. Ron Hubbard's Scientology with the exception that in his doctrine, the UFOs look just like DC-8s). But, within that same twenty minutes she'd counter-contended that she was simply spending too much time online and was clearly swayed by the images in jest that catapulted the temple into outerspace. And just before that roughly twenty minutes was up she'd made a promise to herself that once she left Bangkok she'd regulate her online time.

Ambivalent, or maybe just exhausted from the day's thoughts and chatter on meditation, Styrene flipped open a small, yet thick, formatted book, roughly the size of an over-sized brick that had been sitting beside her. It reproduced a large selection of works by the American artist Ed Ruscha. The text, I WAS GASPING FOR CONTACT, blankly stared back at her in white bold capital letters set slightly at an angle against a muted ground of pastel, laid down in a concentric color wash: reddish in tone at its center radiating out into violet toned grays, darkest in the corners.[37] After staring at it intensely, or intently, for a few minutes Styrene sent the Gold Farmer an instant message "I was gasping for contact." There was no reply, at least not immediately.[38]

37 There was really no way of telling that the work was done in pastel from the mediocre reproduction in the Phaidon 'flip' book. She looked it up in the index of works. To its advantage the book was without addendum texts—and contained only reproductions of Ruscha's works, an index of works and their associative details, in extremely fine print, the publishing information, the slightest biography and one quote by the artist: "Sometimes found words are the most pure because they have nothing to do with you. I take things as I find them. A lot of these things come from the noise of everyday life."
38 Which was the whole point behind instant messaging Styrene would always say, yet of course the only control over such (or said) instantaneity was in its encoding and that itself was relative.

*Flipping Through Ed Ruscha*, 2013, Digital Photograph of a reproduction of Ed Ruscha's *I Was Gasping For Contact*, 1976, Pastel on Paper, Private Collection; in Ed Ruscha, *They Called Her Styrene*, London: Phaidon Press Limited, 2000.

She'd known that she was going to cut ties with the Gold Farmer as soon as she left Bangkok. The whole encounter, or rather obsession, had seemed to become a part of the virtual space she'd mainly inhabited while residing in Bangkok. And while it could continue on anywhere, Styrene had somehow localized it, as it became a necessary condition of being in Bangkok, as it was the activity Styrene had given over her time to and, more accurately, had given over to Judith. It was more likely this fact above all else that was responsible for Styrene's laying Judith to rest than it was an issue of boredom.[39]

She'd still not heard from him yet and was only slightly concerned; it was a rather opaque message and after the last assignment, maybe he was gasping for the antithesis. She hadn't planned on formally cutting off ties but rather 'letting' him figure it out and she thought her last assignment would constitute a poetic goodbye, which at the same time was a ridiculous pathos, a parody on the whole situation. The last assignment she'd given him was rather oblique; it was an excerpt from Eugene Delacroix's journals to be analyzed or commented upon (to 'test' the condition of translation and comprehension). Given art had entered their dialogue, and the Gold Farmer had expressed interest in it and in Western history and culture in general, the assignment, or excerpt, didn't seem too far out of the realm of plausibility or possibility. The assignment was simple only in its complexity, the latter being a condition of the challenge in language—it's borders and (in)translatability.

---

39  And here, Styrene was still quite keen on the reference(s), and her ironic twist of her art history and avatars as though it were somehow avant or garde, though certainly not both.

*While I was sitting in the forest, this morning, I began to think of those charming allegories of the Middle Ages and the Renaissance—those cities of God and bright Elysian fields with their gracious inhabitants, etc. Was not this always the tendency in periods when belief in a higher power retained its full strength? In such times, men's souls strove ceaselessly to escape from trivial anxieties or the sufferings of their actual lives, by seeking some imaginary abode, which they embellished with everything they lacked on earth.*

\*　\*　\*

Although she'd only just introduced herself to Coy, Styrene was hoping that through the relation of a mutual friend, who'd failed to even pass on her name, she'd somehow be allowed to curl up and disappear into sleep within the long narrow burgundy davenport situated beneath the bank of windows until her flight boarded the following early morning. It'd be no problem, "it's a community oriented place," the relation had suggested and she, the relation, was probably accurate yet as dusk fell the space began to fill up rather than empty.

There was growing chatter and Styrene kept hearing the word "gold farmers" bandied about and then finally inquired to the last figure from whom she'd heard the utterance. As it turned out they were going to be screening a recently produced documentary about gold farming exploring the revolution of this emergent industry and its shadow politics and economy.[40] She'd understood that the documentary was shot mostly in China and comprised interviews and documentation with those at work.

While it was mostly inconceivable that Judith's Gold Farmer would have been cast in the documentary the thought of the proper name becoming generic and projected upon a sampling of faces was not a representation she wanted to inhabit, it was better left immaterial. Thus in response to the impending projection, Styrene gathered her belongings and gave up her place (with its free wifi), tucked the book Coy had given her, Bifo's *After the Future*,[41] under her arm and trickled down the four steep narrow stairwells to manage her way to the airport—another, albeit material, non-place she could withstand and lean forward.

40 That this may constitute an obvious way of ending, albeit a tidy one, is a wholly accepted and acknowledged fault. If it is any consolation, the story had hoped to not end here nor end in such a manner yet within its constraints, two of which compete for attention—that of a timing out with a compendium of voices yet to be coalesced—thus accept our apologies, and check out this independent work on gold farming (http://chinesegoldfarmers.com/).

41 The seemingly, or obvious, pretentious reference is a nuisance, but clearly not a nuisance enough to not make the reference. It stands only because the text was heading towards a reference to be made and expanded upon in an attempt to weave the many various immaterial presentations existing here, in-between places of fact and fiction, together, or at least that's how Styrene would justify it. Although, from another perspective, one could argue it was simply already out-accelerated anyhow, already a relic of the present to be overlooked, unless it is still lingering in the slowness of its pause—*in-between* (it just lent itself so easily to cite the title, and relation, again; our apologies).

Jennifer Hope Davy is an artist and writer whose work moves between the poetic and the parodic, largely operating in the form of a gesture, an act or a proposition. She was born and raised primarily in Jersey (New Jersey). She has studied, worked and wandered in various countries across the globe and is now currently in situ. Davy received her Fine Arts degree from the San Francisco Art Institute, her Masters in Art History and Criticism from the University of Texas San Antonio and completed her PhD at the European Graduate School (EGS), where she is currently a post-doctoral fellow, focusing on contemporary art as an apparatus of mobility within aporetic junctures. Forthcoming are the books, *Staging Aporetic Potential,* and *[Given, If, Then]: a reading in three parts.* In addition to art and writing, Davy has functioned as a critic, curator, editor, producer and professor of art and media studies.

www.ingramcontent.com/pod-product-compliance
Lightning Source LLC
Chambersburg PA
CBHW041928010726
47507CB00003BA/220